Sabine and the Silver Hammer

Assisted Sinning
Book 1

Charlotte Northeast

Cover Art by Fers

@thefangomaster

Printed in the USA

First edition, 2025

ISBN - 978-1-968357-11-5

Dedicated to anyone who ever thought love wasn't in the cards. You're never too old to find it....

Also from Trashcan Publishing

- **BOOKMARK FOR THE HEART** by Charlotte Northeast - Small Town Talk, Book 1
- **CARTEL BOMBSHELL** by Didi Pounder
- **RED HOT BLACKTOP** by Didi Pounder
- **DOWN FOR THE COUNT** by Ailis Elliot

Chapter 1

Moving In Day

"Where do you want these?" the burly mover barked, his neck muscles bulging like the roots of the banyan tree standing near the driveway. His arms were laden with an impossibly high number of boxes.

Sabine stopped for a second to admire this display of sweaty strength until she realized he was actually waiting for an answer.

"Uhh," she stammered, a bead of perspiration trickling down the small of her back, "Just there would be fine."

She indicated a corner of what might be... the dining room? She wasn't sure. If anyone asked—which, thankfully, no one had so far—she had no idea if this would be the dining room. It could be a yoga studio for all she knew. Or a place to make pottery. Or a writing den. Or a million other things.

The truth was, she was overwhelmed and exhausted. As much as she'd prepared—carefully packing, making list after list, and even making a vision board just like she'd seen in a wellness magazine—she felt utterly incapable of making the simplest decisions.

She'd always had a partner to help her make such decisions before. Colin had been her rock; a steady presence to help her navigate life's speed bumps. But now this move —and the house that welcomed her—was entirely her own. She had to make all the choices.

Whether she wanted to or not.

"Mmmkay," the mover grunted, easily slinging the boxes down. A faint thud of something inside sent Sabine's frayed nerves twitching into a frenzy, but she decided against investigating further.

It can wait, she said to herself, gritting her teeth.

Stepping aside so he could move past her to the box truck waiting outside, Sabine forced herself to look across the lawn. The back end of the truck was open, and all of Sabine's worldly possessions were in the process of being vomited out.

Wrinkling her nose at such a thought, she pulled at the stray strawberry-blonde hairs sticking to her sweaty neck. Sure, there was some gray in there, but age had caught up to her in the oddest of ways. Her knees creaked at times, and menopause had been a journey she'd much rather forget, but for a woman squarely in her mid-60s, she was in good shape.

Her regular Pilates sessions and power walks helped keep her magically fitting into her favorite jeans and dresses. She wasn't vain, but she sure was finicky about her figure.

For an old widow, I'm not that bad, she thought to herself, hoping the meager pep talk would fight off the rising feeling of despair as each box and piece of furniture was brought in and unceremoniously dumped into whatever empty space the movers could find.

Apparently, they had given up asking her for guidance.

They had deemed her too distracted—or perhaps too old—for the task.

Strangely, she didn't mind. She had nothing but time to sort everything out once the team left.

This is the beginning of the rest of my life, she quipped, not quite believing the chipper tone.

After all, it was hard to believe in something you didn't plan for.

She wasn't supposed to be here at Star Light Senior Village—a sprawling, multi-acre collection of rancher-style houses and cottages laid out over immaculate lawns and criss-crossed by walking paths and golf cart trails.

At the top of a modest hill stood a large, central building housing a gym, community center, retail shop, dining area, and game rooms. It was dressed to look like a white plantation-style house; a large wraparound porch dotted with rocking chairs and side tables. Residents ambled from the color-coded library shelves to shuffling games of bingo, all seemingly content that their lives had brought them to this. Catered to by a staff of largely invisible—and much younger—humans.

The amenities and splendor covered up one very simple truth. That, for most of Star Light's residents, this would be the last place most people would ever live. So why not spend it in luxury?

However, things weren't always luxurious. Often, health issues started to take their toll. Star Light made sure to cater to those needs as well. Tucked discreetly behind the central building was another structure that most people tried to ignore—until they couldn't.

Star Light was billed as a 'resort catering to those in the second act of their lives'—a phrase meant to calm people selling off their family homes and giving up lawn work. A place where you were encouraged to make friends and ignore the outside world. Star Light had it all. Why leave?

The building behind the beating communal heart of the place was just as necessary, though everyone who lived in the village hoped they'd never need it. Part hospital, part rehabilitation center. State of the art and staffed with medical personnel selected for their shiny appearance as much as their medical pedigrees.

And here I am too, Sabine said to herself as she leaned against the window frame of what was definitely her kitchen. At least that was easy to nail down. All the other rooms had infinite possibilities, but the one with the refrigerator and stove made it pretty clear.

Her house faced west, giving her magnificent views of the sunset. Rolling lawns sprawled away from her, only occasionally broken up by another neat rancher.

Star Light was populated, to be sure, but it did try to be exclusive.

Where other villages packed them in, Star Light was more selective.

Sabine felt comforted and guilty all at once.

"Oh, Colin. Can you believe it?" she muttered, flinching at the thump of something heavy—possibly her curio cabinet—being hauled in.

She was sure that Colin would not have believed her new surroundings. Any more than she did.

Yet here she was. And there was no Colin to help her or even marvel at the views.

She never thought she'd move from their comfortable bungalow in the artsy part of town with its sprawling kitchen. She'd spent hours in it experimenting with various cuisines. The overstuffed office where Colin kept all his history books seemed an ideal place to land after retirement.

She'd spent her working years as a beloved middle school social studies teacher, occasionally veering into extracurricular activities like coaching the debate team or hosting the model UN. She had never married—it had just never happened for her—until she met Colin at a mutual friend's party.

Mistaking his drink for hers, they had exchanged numbers within mere moments, the sparks obvious to everyone. Six months later, she had moved in with him, marveling at his wine collection and his tendency to surprise her with last minute travel plans.

A blissful six years passed in a flash, but it all came to a crashing halt when a growth was discovered on Colin's kidney. Within six months, he was gone, leaving a hole so deep in Sabine's life, she never thought she'd be able to climb out again.

But Colin—despite his tendency to seem compulsive—was a true planner at heart. Sabine was shocked to her core when she was told how Colin had taken care of her financially.

"You got some nice stuff, lady," one of the movers blurted, shaking Sabine out of her reverie. "It was a... uhhh... pleasure to move you today."

He stood, his ragged baseball cap in his hands, obviously put up by the others on his team to play nice with the doddering old lady in an effort to get a healthy tip.

It worked. Sabine could never display any backbone when it came to tipping. Colin had always taken care of that.

One more thing I have to get used to, Sabine reminded herself as she foraged in her purse for some cash.

Palming it, the man tipped his hat and clomped out.

Within minutes, she heard the clang of a metal door and the roar of an engine.

Silence filled the vacuum, reminding Sabine how utterly alone she was now.

In her new house.

Its single tenant.

A nauseating anxiety crept up the back of Sabine's throat, its itchy fingers pulling at her eyelids. She knew if she gave into it, she might end up in a sobbing heap on the floor.

Who knows the last time that's been cleaned? a voice inside her head cautioned.

Taking a halting breath, she tried to heave herself into the shape of someone who needed to locate the glassware, that lone bottle of wine she knew she packed, and possibly the corkscrew.

Hell, if needs must, she'd just bust the thing open on the kitchen counter.

She didn't get the chance.

"Knock, knock," a cheery voice sounded out.

Sabine's mood flashed from pity party to annoyed in the blink of an eye.

Who says 'knock, knock' when they could actually just knock?

Still, she needed to put on a brave face, so she called out, "Hello!" and headed to the front door. Which was surprisingly still open. Even after receiving a tip, she thought the movers would have at least closed the door behind them.

Guess it's not something they do a whole lot in their line of work, she mused sarcastically.

Standing there, blocking the yolk-yellow globs of sun that filtered down in the decaying afternoon light, was a stout woman with a dated hairstyle—think 1980s bowling alley chic—wearing ill-fitting navy slacks and one of those blouses that resembled a child's crayon explosion drawing.

"Hi there! Welcome to the neighborhood! I'm Debbie Carruthers! The Activities Coordinator here at Star Light! It's my absolute pleasure to make you feel at home here!"

"Oh... uh... hi," Sabine said, wondering if Debbie was going to start showing her how to crochet that very second. She sincerely hoped not.

"Settling in, I see?" Debbie craned her neck inside the foyer, her beady brown eyes no doubt assessing the value of the few objects that weren't encased in cardboard. Sabine got the queasy feeling that Debbie had one persona as Activities Coordinator and quite another when she was at home. Debbie's eye had the appraising look of an experienced pawnbroker.

"Uhh... yes, I suppose. The movers just left, so, you know... *lots* to do," Sabine replied, in a tone that she hoped conveyed a sense of being polite with a hint of 'you can go now' sprinkled lightly on the top.

"Oh, I'm sure," Debbie said, waving a hand with an alarming safety-cone-orange set of acrylic nails. "But you've got *tons* of time to do that. Why don't you take a little break and come on over to the comm center?"

Sabine blinked.

"The what?"

Debbie giggled. She was way too old to be giggling, but there it was.

"Oh, there I go. Being silly and expecting you to know things. The Comm Center. The *Community* Center. It's the beating heart of Star Light. *Everyone* goes there." She leaned close, laying a conspiratorial hand on Sabine's forearm. Sabine instantly regretted her life choices.

Debbie's voice dropped low. "It's where lasting friendships are made."

Does she know she talks like a pamphlet? Sabine wondered.

She didn't have time to ponder it much further. Debbie stood her ground (a formidable patch of it with a wide-legged stance), and Sabine knew that 'no' wasn't an option.

"Uhhhh… sure, let me just grab my keys and purse."

Debbie smiled. A smile of victory. One that Sabine realized she probably made often. Debbie had the air of someone who usually got her way.

"Excellent," Debbie replied breezily. "You won't regret it. It's important to get to know the other residents."

Sabine closed the door ruefully and followed Debbie up the path.

She sighed as she did so. Debbie—in many ways—was right. What if these were the last friendships she ever made?

Chapter 2

Welcome Wagon

"**W**e're not walking?" Sabine asked as Debbie slid her large rear end into the golf cart waiting at the top of the path.

"Oh no! Here at Star Light, we golf cart," Debbie proclaimed, patting the empty seat next to her.

Sabine smiled and climbed in, her movements not nearly as graceful as Debbie's.

Another thing to get used to. Also, is 'golf cart' supposed to be viewed as a verb?

Golf carts don't go very fast, but that didn't mean Debbie didn't try. With a lead foot, the cart lurched to top speed within seconds, and Sabine gripped the thin pole that held up the front of the roof. She tried not to grit her teeth.

The expanse that was Star Light rolled by, the scent of citrus and grass clippings wafting in from every side. The place was immaculate, and Sabine recalled her initial tour of the place.

Pockets of land dotted with small, neat, single floor homes, the obligatory American flags, and bright flowers peeping from every lawn.

She'd been in a daze when she first explored the grounds, but so impressed with the feeling of ease and tranquility, she had signed on the dotted line that same day.

It didn't hurt that her house was a tad more secluded than the others and had a fantastic view.

"This *just* came on the market," the saleswoman had purred. "Very new."

Sabine had tried not to think too deeply about what that meant. Easy to do given that the saleswoman—Trudy might have been her name—was wearing enough perfume to fumigate a warehouse.

Sabine had moved back as far as she could without looking impolite and grabbed her pen to sign the proffered papers.

If it just became available then that means someone just...

"And we're here!" Debbie proclaimed, snapping Sabine out of her second grim daydream of the day. Shaking her head, Sabine reminded herself to stay focused. She needed her wits about her if she was going to figure this place out. Since she couldn't rely on Colin to do it...

A pang of heartache zapped through her like an electrical wire, and she froze momentarily.

"Hellooooo? You okay?" Debbie chirped. She had hopped out of the cart but was now leaning back in, her face close to Sabine, who hadn't moved.

"Uhh... yes. Sorry. The day is catching up to me, I guess," Sabine stammered, forcefully packing her pain into a tiny square and shoving it into the corner of her heart.

Debbie's confusion eased, and she backed away. If she clocked Sabine's distress, she sure wasn't wasting any time dealing with it. Debbie had other things to do.

"Alrighty! Here we go!"

Following behind like a dutiful puppy, they entered the Community Center. The sliding doors opened silently, and a whiff of cooked meat and fresh flowers made Sabine's nose wrinkle briefly before she became nose-blind.

The place was wonderfully cool but not cold—that magic temperature that people over the age of 65 can never seem to find.

Maybe this was another reason I chose the place? Sabine thought, trying to keep pace with Debbie's large strides. Briefly, Sabine marveled at the shortness of Debbie's legs versus the large strides she took. Quickly, though, her attention was needed elsewhere.

"Games and crafts take place over there," Debbie said, pointing down a hallway. Sabine could barely keep up. "Here's the main dining area. I know you know all this from your initial tour, but it can never hurt to have a refresher..." she stated, her orange nails like flags. "The theater is down there. They do some wonderful productions."

Sabine's eyes followed Debbie's hands, trying to memorize it all.

"And here," Debbie proclaimed, finally coming to a stop inside a large central chamber, "is the where it all happens—The Hub."

They stood in the entrance of a large, circular space, decorated with navy blue carpeting and cream walls. Comfortable yet bland-colored chairs and small tables created conversation zones, where people talked, played cards, or read.

Standing sentinel over the whole room was a large, oculus-like window, the sun benevolently shining in from above. The room felt cavernous and lived in all at once. A strange combination. Sabine tried not to think too deeply about what her experience of this room might be.

Debbie sucked air into her lungs like she was standing at the top of a mountain. Turning to Sabine, she looked her dead in the eyes. Sabine took an involuntary step back. The moment felt... *momentous* somehow, like Debbie was going to say something that would change Sabine's life forever.

"This is where pals are made," Debbie intoned, as if she had said something worthy of the Dalai Lama.

Sabine deflated a little but tried to nod reverently, her eyes scanning the knots of people milling about.

After a short pause, Debbie continued. "There, those ladies right there. They are the ones to *know*."

Without waiting for Sabine to follow her eyes, Debbie was off again, heading towards a gaggle of women who dominated the center areas of the room. At first, Sabine couldn't make out much detail. It seemed to her to be a moving, flowing organism made up of purplish white hair, pastel blouses, and jangling silver bracelets.

It was, in short, a group of women clad in expensive (if slightly garish) clothes and far too much makeup.

Now, now, Sabine warned herself. *What did I used to tell my students? 'Replace judgment with curiosity?'*

And curious she was. These women, who, as she approached, became more distinct as singular beings rather than a moving kerfuffle of gesticulating arms and flashing acrylic nails, were certainly colorful and intriguing.

Besides, Sabine had no choice. Debbie was heading straight towards them.

Somehow, without thinking too much about it, Sabine's feet plodded behind Debbie, caught in the wake of her tractor beam.

"...I'm telling you, he had *two* fake knees and one fake hip. Didn't stop him from—oh hello, Debbie!" one of the women chirruped, halting whatever salacious gossip she was dishing out. The other women fluttered in response, some hiding their laughter behind their hands, others flashing knowing glances at each other.

The woman who was speaking appeared nonplussed by the whole thing. Sabine got the distinct impression she hadn't stopped speaking out of shame, but rather because whatever she was sharing was curated. That only a chosen few would be privy to whatever lurid factoid she was about to spill.

And—it was obvious to Sabine—Debbie hadn't made the cut.

Noted.

In her periphery, Sabine noticed a distinct change in Debbie's demeanor. A few minutes prior, Debbie had seemed solid—a woman who took up space and was proud to do so. Now she seemed fidgety, flighty; her body trembled a little, her hands tremored in front of her midsection, and her orange nails flapped disconcertingly.

"Oh, hello, Grace! So great to run into you! I was—" Debbie gushed, her voice thin and reedy.

That's new, Sabine added to her list of observations.

"Yes, Debbie. I saw the flyer. I'll *think* about it, okay?" Grace said, her tone at once condescending and saccharine. The women surrounding Grace pursed their lips in stilted laughter.

A creeping, acidic sensation rippled through Sabine's stomach. A sense-memory she had long forgotten. Tamping it down, she focused on Debbie.

"Oh great! I just know that you would bring down the house! The Players need you for the lead," Debbie continued, her hands still flapping.

"We'll see. It all might be in the way of my *procedure*," Grace replied, stringing out this last word. Sabine got the impression this was meant to show that whatever Grace was having done was elective and fabulous and not something life threatening or embarrassing like a toenail removal.

That would track, Sabine said, giving Grace a thorough look. The woman was willowy and tall, her bony shoulders encased in a silk peach blouse with sky blue slacks. Her hair was a wavy construction of loose curls falling to her shoulders, and she had the kind of cheekbones that Sofia Loren could be jealous of.

If she wore makeup, it was subtle and tasteful, her muted palette differing from the wild colors and pastel explosions of the women that surrounded her.

Her entourage, Sabine realized, the acidic feeling returning with a vengeance.

"Right, right," Debbie replied, disappointment curling her words. Then, turning to Sabine, she said, "Sabine Wilcox, this is Grace Pickney and these are her friends, known around here as the Golden Graces. The GGs. If you want to know anything about Star Light, they are the ones to ask!" Debbie leaned in, like a bad impression of a conspirator, and added, "beyond our excellent staff, that is!"

Sabine smiled wanly, hoping this chummy routine would be over soon. She was getting a little buzzy. Between the move, the shock of relocating, and Debbie's forced field trip, the day was starting to catch up to her.

"Pleasure," Grace purred, though she didn't extend a hand. "This is Rebecca, Ginny, Topaz, and Helen," Grace said, her other dancer-like hand waving vaguely at other women. They nodded in turn, and Sabine did her best to assign names to faces but quickly realized it was a losing game.

They looked interchangeable. White skin, bright clothes, steely gazes.

Hooooo-boy, Sabine thought, reminding herself again not to judge too quickly.

"Nice to meet you all," Sabine said, surprising herself with how automatic the reply came out of her.

Grace's laser-beam gaze looked Sabine up and down. After an agonizing second, she moved her gray-green eyes from Sabine to Debbie. Debbie reacted like a plant starving for water, her whole body leaning forward.

"I'll take a look at the dates again and get back to you. When are auditions?" Grace asked.

Debbie almost squealed in pleasure.

"Oh, not until next week. But I'm sure Jerrold won't make you go through all that. He knows talent when he sees it. Just let me know and I'll make it happen. You'll be an excellent Blanche!"

For all her dismissiveness, Grace couldn't resist taking the unadulterated compliment.

"Mmmm, yes," she replied, basking in the echo of affirming nods from the rest of the Graces.

The next few seconds ticked by in silence. Sabine could feel Debbie's enjoyment at Grace's attentions, and Grace seemed to want Debbie to make her exit.

For her part, Sabine had no idea what her role in all of this was supposed to be. Suddenly, she longed for her cluttered, disorganized house with deep urgency.

'Well," Debbie said, finally filling the seconds with sound, "I should be on my way. *So much* to do to make Star Light a fun place to be!"

Again with the pamphlet-speak, Sabine reflected.

"Uh-uh," came Grace's bored reply.

If Debbie hoped to have yet more of Grace's attention, she was sorely mistaken. Grace lowered herself into a chair, picking up a small, intricate purse. Rummaging through it for her compact, her attention was trained on only one person—her own reflection.

With a slight sigh, Debbie finally got the hint.

"Okay. Y'all have fun now! Play nice!" Debbie crooned, giving Sabine a wink before leaving the group behind.

Sabine watched Debbie's broad backside weave through the room, occasionally stopping to pep-talk more Star Light residents. Slowly, though, Sabine knew she had to turn back to her new... acquaintances.

Maybe they will smile and make some silly joke about Debbie and we can be friends, Sabine thought, trying to manifest it into being.

It's not like she *needed* friends. She had plenty from her old life. Friends she could call up anytime and send letters and packages too whenever she wished.

But they don't live here. I can't see them every day.

The acidic feeling returned a third time, this time tinged with a strange kind of homesickness.

A homesickness for her old life.

One she had *willingly* given up to move here.

Face your new friends. Smile. Play along, Sabine coaxed herself, suddenly realizing the last time she'd felt this acrid anxiety in her guts.

Middle school. It was in middle school. Decades ago.

She turned and faced the group. She wished for smiling faces and warm welcomes.

Instead, she got frosty glances and pointed looks of disdain in return.

Sabine's eyes moved from face to face, searching for something friendly like a port in a storm.

Glare from Helen. Derision from Topaz. Disdain from Rebecca. Something akin to disgust from Ginny.

But it was Grace that was the most disconcerting. A look of hunger. A look of something almost predatory.

"Silly Debbie. We *always* play nice, don't we, girls?" Grace mused, her nails clicking on the chair's armrest.

Sabine's stomach tilted and swayed.

Yup. Middle school. All over again.

It was hardly the welcome she had been expecting.

In point of fact, it wasn't a welcome at all.

Chapter 3

Just Passing Through

"Annnnnddddd... in she goes! Smooth as silk," Dennis crooned, leaning on his putter, his dentures gleaming with an unnatural luster. "You owe me another ten-spot, Crenshaw."

The assembled crowd—all men, all lounging on chairs or against walls, hooted, and applauded Dennis' latest putting victory—a sunk shot from the longest distance the indoor green could offer.

All cheered but one—Felix Crenshaw. The one who had bet big (at least by indoor putting in the afternoon standards) and had lost.

"Not my day today," Felix replied, pushing aside the wedge of silver hair that perpetually tried to shield his left eye.

He smiled as he spoke, portraying a sunny demeanor— every bit the picture of a man who could lose with grace, even a sense of humor.

Inside, though, he was irritated. A jagged itch in his chest.

Dennis—in his salmon-pink pants and turquoise blue

polo, stretched over a round belly—represented everything Felix had wanted to escape in retirement. Loud, boisterous, privileged men who did their best to make everything a competition and loudly proclaimed their triumphs, no matter how inconsequential, whenever they got the chance.

Felix was certain that if situations were reversed, Dennis would not be so gracious in defeat.

"Well, you can't win 'em all. Hey—with your good looks, I bet you win in all sorts of other ways, right?" Dennis said, leaning in close and elbowing Felix. "I bet the ladies all want a piece of your 'silver hammer,' don't they?"

Felix wanted to swat Dennis' leering eyebrows right off his forehead. He hated that nickname. He couldn't even remember how it had started, but once it was in the air, the golf guys used it as often as they could. Felix just wanted the ordeal to be over, so he simply shrugged and gave a half smile.

Dennis continued, "Pay up then! This is how you earn your stripes here at Camp Star Light," Dennis bellowed, basking in the nods and whoops in return from the men around him.

Lemmings, all of them, Felix thought bitterly before reminding himself to calm down.

Truth was, these weren't bad guys, really. They were simply enjoying a few golden moments away from their partners—girlfriends or wives—where they could let loose a little.

So much of life at Star Light was built around activities and being social. For people who had worked most of their lives, this was a hard assignment—especially since wives and girlfriends expected their men to be around more. That special brand of all-the-time kind of more.

Felix could easily see that it wore some of them down,

causing them to form whatever bonds with the other men they could. Bonds they held onto for dear life.

And yet, this is where Felix struggled. Having no partner, he was unfettered and could travel about as he pleased. While there were other single people at Star Light, they were mostly women. Those other single men that managed to make it this far into their senior years were often—as Felix could absolutely attest—either unappealing or downright anti-social.

Felix knew he was a rarity, and while that might have been helpful outside of Star Light, here it was akin to wearing a billboard that said "single, older man—take pity or invade personal space as you wish!"

Maybe I should have stayed in my condo, Felix mused, as he handed over a crisp $10 bill to Dennis, who pocketed it instantly.

Not that Dennis needed the money. From what Felix had heard, Dennis used to be a big-time businessman; made a fortune in the sale of pool chemicals or some other venture. Felix hadn't bothered to pay much attention.

"Another go?" Dennis asked, his tongue sliding across his bottom lip in a disconcerting display of male prowess. His brown eyes sparkled with a surprisingly youthful quality. The rest of Dennis' face was leathery from a life spent on golf courses.

"Not today, I'm afraid. I'm a little thirsty," Felix replied, adding a friendly clap on Dennis' shoulder to show he was still a good sport.

Dennis was solid and square. Felix had a few inches on him, and his own toned body looked far better in linen pants and a lightweight, short-sleeved summer shirt.

"Awww, you'll have better luck next time, Felix old pal,"

Dennis said, his faux condescension pulling more laughter from the onlookers.

"Maybe," Felix said, "maybe..."

He drifted away as Dennis threw out a challenge to his next competitor.

It was all so... familiar. This elaborate game of social standing and one-upmanship, all under the guise of being "friendly" and "approachable."

Felix supposed there was a chance of a real friendship here, but after six months at Star Light, he had yet to find it.

Thoughts of his airy condo up North floated into his brain as he headed to the Comm Center to seek out a drink, but the winters had convinced him that moving to the South was his only option for staying sane. Snow, sleet, and a bum knee due to a long-ago skiing incident urged him to sell up and move to Star Light. He still struggled to swallow the bitter realization he was becoming a stereotype—the permanent snowbird, willingly trapped in a lush paradise—complete with dining options and amenities such as indoor putting greens and bingo nights.

As he strode down the hall, nodding to staff and residents alike, he tried to push the thought away—*he was here*. He had invested in a pretty house with a full golf membership, and now he had to make the most of it.

His sandals made a pleasing slapping sound on the carpet as he walked. Nursing a hope that the staff had put out his favorite drink—their signature blueberry lemonade— he arrived in the southern doorway of the Comm Center.

As usual, the place was busy with games of Scrabble in one corner, pockets of people talking in another, and some with younger family members or friends visiting. The Comm Center was the bustling center of it all, complete with a snack table and plenty of drink options.

His eyes scanned the large counter area against one wall where the drinks were placed, and his mood rose. There was the pitcher—glistening with condensation—and a phalanx of tall glasses waiting patiently nearby.

Okay, maybe life here isn't so bad, Felix thought, turning his steps in that direction. Without realizing it, his lips parted, his tongue running over his top teeth in anticipation of the cool, slightly bittersweet drink...

"Felix! Ohhhhh, Felix!"

He froze in place, his mouth dried, and his heart sank.

Damnit. The GGs.

A knot of frustration formed in his stomach. He had been foolish to walk into the Comm Center in the middle of the day. Felix should have known the GGs would be here, their hyena laughs, pawing hands, and coquettish routines on full display.

Objectively speaking, he knew they were among the most attractive women here—they took good care of their bodies and made a considerable effort each time they left their houses. All the same, their laughter sounded like braying, they had nothing in the way of conversation skills, and they looked at him the same way he looked at the blueberry lemonade—with abject longing.

It was... off-putting to say the least.

But not bad for the ego, a voice reminded him. That one honest voice in his head he tried to quell early and often.

After briefly considering whether to pretend he hadn't seen or heard them (only a blind and deaf man could have possibly missed their effusive display), he reluctantly turned in their direction. The eyes of others outside the orbit of the GGs passed over him as he walked, some with outright daggers of jealousy. To be summoned by the GGs was something many people craved, while others shot him looks of pity or even a sense of smug triumph at being spared their attention.

Within moments, he was swallowed into their group, tethered until he could find a reasonable excuse to get away.

"There you are!" Grace Pickney thrummed, her willowy arm linking into his before he had a chance to object. "Where have you been, stranger?"

"Ah, nowhere," he said. "Golfing, mostly."

Grace playfully rolled her eyes and swatted at him. The others—Felix recalled their names but couldn't tell you which name belonged to which woman—smiled and nodded, doing their best approximation of shy girls.

You're women of a certain age. Act like it! a voice commended in Felix's mind. He hoped his face didn't betray the notion.

"Golfing?! I'll never understand men's fascination with that game. Especially on the same course—over and over. How dull!" Grace whinnied, playing it up for Felix's benefit.

"I enjoy it. As for playing the same course over and over—it's a lot like chess. The repetition is what makes it fascinating."

Felix wasn't sure where this little speech had come from, but there it was, and it momentarily stumped Grace. Her coral-lipsticked lips parted for a moment as she scanned his face for clues. His gray-blue eyes looked back, a stoic, unreadable expression playing across his angular features.

"Ah, yes. I suppose. I wouldn't know anything about that." She briskly changed the subject. "So, have you learned to put down your lawyering tools and simply enjoy yourself yet? If not, I have *plenty* of ideas to help you."

"She really does," Helen piped in, her eagerness

apparent. Grace shot her a look of approval mixed with a command of 'shut up and know your place.' Helen shut her mouth.

"You're new here? So am I," came a voice. One that didn't belong to Grace, Helen, or any of the rest. All the heads in the group turned to see who it was.

A woman in a slightly rumpled shirt and jeans looked directly at Felix, her silvering strawberry-blonde hair pulled in a hasty bun on top of her head. Her expression was open and vulnerable, and Felix had the distinct notion that this was a terrible thing to be. In this place. With this company.

He wanted to get out of there even more.

"Uh, yes. Six months." He put his hands in his pockets, extricating himself from Grace's grip. "Excuse me, everyone. I have to be going. Have a phone call..." he said, voice low.

"Oh no!" Grace protested. "You only just got here! We never see you! You're like Star Light's ghost!"

"I don't mind ghosts," Felix retorted, taking the wind out of Grace's sails. "Have a lovely rest of your day, ladies. As lovely as all of you are." He mimed tipping a hat to them all—enjoying the flutter of blushes that resulted—and turned towards the drink station.

The resulting prize felt hollow, though. The unique taste seemed somewhat dulled.

Still, Felix was glad to have kept his interaction with the GGs short. And yes—he had to admit to himself that their attentions were flattering, but one nagging thought remained, even as he took a glass and headed outside.

Who was that mystery woman, and why had she looked at him like that?

Chapter 4

Traffic Laws

"Thought you could take on Felix, did you?" Grace had asked, her question biting and ice-cold. "No one can get through to that man. Believe me, I've tried. You would do well... not to try."

The GGs murmured in agreement, their faces mirroring their leader's.

Sabine at once felt she had committed two sins—one, the dire sin of daring to start a conversation like an adult, and two, challenging the societal hierarchy here at Star Light.

Apparently, both were enough to get her into the kind of hot water where she now swam.

Despite her inner voices screaming out to the contrary, Sabine persisted.

"Oh, I was just wondering about his story... how he—"

Grace held up a delicate hand—at once fragile and cutting.

"Felix is a man that doesn't wish to be bothered. He's made that clear. Don't even try."

Back off is what you really mean, Sabine thought to

herself. Grace was showing the bright line of the boundary —something Sabine had just crossed.

Felix was a mystery. A paradox. And he was devilishly handsome—his gray-blue eyes witty and sharp.

Which meant he was off limits. Especially to someone like Sabine.

Sabine's throat went dry, but she managed to speak— just enough to get out of there.

"Got it. Thanks for telling me," she stammered.

Grace smiled superciliously and returned to her friends, already moving on to the next piece of gossip. Now that they were distracted, Sabine made a hasty exit.

Try not to judge. Try not to judge. Try not to— Sabine repeated the mantra over and over to herself as she retreated from the Comm Center. It even rankled that she had thought of the room where the GGs held court as the Comm Center. It meant that she had tacitly agreed upon the rules here—that she was now part of it.

But she knew she wasn't. The GGs had made that crystal clear. She was not part of their coffee klatch. Their society. Their... cult.

Far from it.

The moment the admittedly handsome but snobbish man had left their group, the GGs had turned their collective attention to her.

The recollection of it—though it had only taken place minutes ago—snagged at her, already a more than painful memory. Veering dangerously close to humiliation.

All the draconian rules of middle school came tumbling back to Sabine in an instant—even as she willed her feet to move faster away from the Comm Center and back to her house.

There, at least, she thought she could busy herself

unpacking. Or just make a nest out of cardboard boxes and live out the rest of her days in it. Surely, she had enough canned food somewhere that meant she wouldn't have to leave her house ever again?

Nonsense! Another voice cried. *Why should you be a prisoner in your own home? You're an adult. You can speak to whomever you like! Even if he's a cold fish.*

Shaking her head, she aimed her feet squarely in the direction of her house, sticking to the broad path that she and Debbie had taken earlier.

Her return, however, was slower-going. Now she was on foot. Not being whisked with retirement village efficiency on a swanky golf cart.

Still, Sabine needed the time and the exercise to think. She had to try to build a life here. Surely there were more people at Star Light like her. Reasonable-minded, friendly people who could carry on a normal conversation without making it into a turf war. Surely, there were men who—while perhaps not as good-looking—might be kinder and more willing to strike up a friendship.

Another stab clenched at her heart. She didn't think that companionship of any kind more than friendship was in her future. After all, Colin had already been a pleasant surprise in her life. Someone she never thought she'd get to know. The six years she spent with him were some of the happiest she'd ever had.

I need to start fresh. That's why I'm here. I can find my people. Remember, it's only the first day.

This thought, combined with the cool, lemon-scented air that wafted over her, calmed her somewhat. She slowed her stride just a touch, allowing the breeze to cool some of the sweat collecting along her hairline. Vaguely, she hoped she'd be able to locate her shower curtain in the boxes so she could take a shower tonight. Moving day had been an exhausting and dusty affair.

"Yes, I'll find my people..." she whispered in an effort to reassure herself. "Maybe."

It almost worked. She almost believed she was totally calm until another thought barged its way in. Stopping short, she replayed the last conversation she'd had with the GGs. What she'd promised before Felix arrived and she scuttled out of there.

Too late, the moments replayed in her mind like a movie.

"Are you good with figures?" Helen had asked, her pointy face—and oddly dyed reddish-brown hair—staring directly at Sabine.

The change of topic was even more jarring in Sabine's memory, no matter how she'd tried her best not to read too much into it. And how the other GGs leaned in, Grace wearing their placid smiles. It had reminded Sabine of a snake sunning itself. She decided to play things cautiously.

"Ummm, do you mean math? That sort of thing? Yes, I suppose so," she replied, thinking back to one of her first jobs in retail as she worked her way through college. "I can run a register if someone shows me how."

Helen clapped precisely once. "Good! We're always looking for volunteers for the store."

"Store?" Sabine asked, a strange feeling growing in her stomach.

"Yes, the store. Just outside the Comm Center here. Open three days a week. Sells clothing, gifts, that sort of thing. We're always looking for people."

Sabine nodded noncommittally, wondering why retired people would set themselves up this way. Aren't they supposed to free themselves from anything resembling work?

"What about artsy stuff? Painting, sewing... generally being useful?" Grace asked, her eyes once again sliding up and down Sabine's body.

"Uhh... yeah. I've been known to do those things..." Sabine said lamely, feeling cornered.

"Wonderful," Grace trilled. "We're in desperate need of volunteers for the theater. Scenic painting, mending. All that. Rehearsals start soon—*Streetcar Named Desire*. I've been asked to be in it by *Debbie*," Grace stopped to enjoy the virulent eye-rolling and sniggering by the other GGs at Debbie's expense, "but I haven't decided yet. You should be a part of it. It's always fun. And a great way to meet people. You're going to love it."

Sabine shook her head, already wincing at the memory. Huffing out a breath, she resumed walking, trying to stuff the GGs flinty looks and smug smiles at having roped another sucker into their orbit.

Another victim. Another... servant, Sabine thought sadly. What had she agreed to, exactly? And what did it all mean?

Her heart clenched and her thoughts whirled, trying to piece it all together, even as her legs walked her home— seemingly on auto pilot.

"Watch out! What the hell?!"

Sabine nearly jumped out of her skin, which manifested as her doing a sort of sideways shuffle off the path and into the grass. Snapping her head, she caught sight of a golf cart coming to an abrupt stop—missing her by mere inches.

The sun sliced down into Sabine's eyes as she turned to face the man behind the wheel—perched on the driver's side. He was a good four feet from Sabine, and the shade of the golf cart's top obscured her full view of him.

He, on the other hand, wasn't about to let obscurity hide his opinions.

"What the hell are you doing? This is a cart path! No pedestrians! Didn't you see the sign?"

Indignation, shame, and exasperation welled up in Sabine—a thorny ball of emotions that threatened to take her voice away. Swallowing hard, she regrouped.

"I'm new here," she protested. "Maybe you don't have to drive like a maniac?" It was a weak argument, and she knew it. It was clear she had to pay more attention and learn the rules of the place—but did he have to be so rude about it?

The man snorted angrily. He leaned forward, the shade dropping from his face, revealing his identity to Sabine.

A knot of anger replaced her earlier feelings. Because of course.

"Maybe you don't belong here, then," he growled, his grey-blue eyes flashing with anger.

Sabine set her jaw, too angry to speak.

Because—starting back at her—was none other than Felix.

Of course. Why would I expect anyone else?

Chapter 5

Time Bandies With Us All

What a jerk! What an absolute jerk! Sabine fumed, her legs blurring as she practically speed-walked back home.

Other, less charitable phrases flashed through her mind.

Like playing with paper dolls, she superimposed each fresh new insult over the image of Felix's rude face jutting out of the golf cart. The ritual felt oddly calming—whipping up her anger while also propping up her bruised ego.

This time, she studiously followed the footpath designed for walkers. Sabine couldn't help but notice it was barely used, almost overgrown with spotty grasses, banyan tree roots, and fallen palm fronds.

"Doesn't anyone walk around here?" she asked aloud, incredulous. Only the chirp of a passing bird answered her.

She'd left Felix in a huff, her only reply to his incredibly rude statement about her not belonging here being a sharp intake of breath and a quick turn on her heel.

She didn't owe him anything—least of all her precious time.

If she could just get home, she could close the door on

these awful people and figure out what to do next. Hell, she had barely unpacked yet, so maybe she could just chuck it all back in a truck and find somewhere else to go.

Sabine knew she was being dramatic, but her nerves were scraped raw, and this seemed like the best way to soothe them.

Maybe today was just a fluke.

Maybe there are nicer people.

Maybe, maybe, maybe...

She wanted so desperately to believe it.

Cresting a small hill, her house came into view, its bare front porch and flagpole yelling to the world that someone new had moved in. Another cookie-cutter house just waiting for some personal touches from its new owner.

For a brief moment, her anger subsided, replaced by thoughts of possibility. That tiny anticipation that comes with starting over. Of allowing hope over what's next.

A split second later, her heart sank as she was confronted with a sight she wasn't expecting.

There in her small driveway was another truck, the driver's side door open. She could just make out the shape of a man's leg sticking out. Someone was waiting for her.

Did the movers forget something?

But no, this truck was different. Smaller and leaner. And it had a different name emblazoned on the side: Second to Noon Clock Repair

Her heart sank further. She was not ready. Not for this.

Taking a gulp of air, she hurried down the path to her house, coming to a stop in front of the driver, who was lounging in his seat squinting over a clipboard.

Another man, squat and disinterested, sat lumpily in the passenger side. A strong whiff of body odor and beef jerky emanated from the messy cab littered with soda bottles and fast food wrappers.

She opened her mouth to speak, but the driver cut her off.

"You Sabine Wilcox?" he asked, his spotty mustache and jagged teeth only adding to the unpleasant feeling Sabine had in her stomach. Returning to her maiden name still jarred her, but with Colin gone being called Sabine Mayhew just didn't sound right. It was too much of a reminder of the man she'd lost.

"Yes," she said gingerly. "Are you here with my grandfather clock?"

"Yeah, we've been here ten minutes. We told you delivery was at 3:15."

Sabine frantically searched her mental calendar.

"I'm sorry. I think there's been a misunderstanding. I didn't receive any notice about this. I was told I would get a call, but that it wouldn't be for at least another week."

The driver didn't seem to want to tackle this piece of information. He was annoyed and intended on fully displaying it.

"I don't know nothing about that. Anyway, we gotta get this thing in your house. You ready or not?"

For a moment, Sabine was too stunned to speak.

How are people so rude these days and yet still employed?

She hired this company to fix one of her prized possessions—a grandfather clock that Colin and she had bought as a gift to each other when they first started getting serious.

She had hoped to have the house in better shape so that when it was delivered, it would be received with grace and care. And, according to the ad and all the customer testimonials, that's what Second to Noon promised.

Yet, here she was, facing a brutal truth: false advertising was a bitch.

Setting her jaw, she said primly, "I suppose so. Follow me."

The driver barked at his companion. "Let's go, Ray."

Ray, exhaling loudly, got out, and the two men opened the back of the truck.

Sabine opened the front door, tamping down the immediate overwhelming sight of all the boxes and objects strewn about by the movers.

Will this day ever end? she lamented.

Blowing stray hairs out of her face, Sabine decided to get this over with and pout about it later. The faster these guys did their thing, the faster she'd be able to slam the door on the world for a while.

The driver—whose name Sabine had failed to get—and Ray were huffing and puffing in the back of the truck. Loud metallic bangs and scrapes could be heard as they lowered the truck's ramp. Sprinkled with rust and mangy with missing paint, the truck had seen better days. Second to Noon wasn't exactly springing for upkeep on its fleet of vehicles, Sabine noted, typing up the scathing Yelp review in her head as she propped the front door open.

A minute or so later, Ray and the driver had managed to manhandle a large object onto a dolly. It was wrapped in frayed bits of cardboard and raggedy bubble wrap. It didn't bear the faintest resemblance to the glossy photos in the ads Sabine had counted on. This monstrosity looked more like a kindergartner's chaotic art project than Sabine's precious grandfather clock.

I should have done more shopping around, Sabine

chastised herself, her foot tapping impatiently as Ray and the driver pulled the dolly along.

Even that effort seemed cavalier, the package listing dangerously to one side on a number of occasions.

"Be careful!" Sabine called out, panic rising in her throat.

The driver looked at her, his eyes flinty with annoyance.

"Yeah, yeah," he replied, waving dismissively. Ray simply rolled his eyes.

Careless AND rude. How are these guys able to stay in business?

Finally, and somehow miraculously, the wretched pair arrived at the door and began to hoist the dolly into the house. Sabine stepped aside, her eyes never leaving them.

With the driver in front and Ray standing behind the dolly, they started to move forward, but a wheel caught on the door jamb.

The driver clucked with irritation.

"Dammit. Ok. On three..." he instructed. "One, two..."

Before he could say 'three,' Ray lunged forward, pushing the dolly. Catching the driver off-guard, he stumbled into the foyer, causing the dolly to tip precariously.

"Wait!" Sabine called out, her hands flying out uselessly in front of her.

The clock made a sickening thudding sound, complete with the sad whimper of the weights and bells as it hit the side of the door jamb.

The driver reached out, grabbing it just before it slid off the dolly entirely.

"We got it, we got it!" he grunted back, venting his anger towards Sabine rather than Ray and his poor timing.

"I'm not sure you do!" Sabine retorted, her anger and frustration spilling out. She couldn't believe these men had been put in charge of such precious objects. As soon as she could, she would be phoning their boss.

"Look, lady—" the driver began, and Sabine could tell she was about to get an earful.

"Just do your job and get out," a voice said, the tone cold and forceful.

Suddenly, all motion stopped as Ray, the driver, and Sabine tried to locate its source. Who just spoke? And why did it have the power to stop everyone in their tracks?

Turning, Sabine had yet another shock—the day was full of them, apparently.

It was Felix, his eyebrows locked in a grimace, his jaw set. He emanated authority and, by his very presence, demanded instant respect.

The driver's mouth—previously curled in anger—morphed into something else: remorse.

"Hey, mister, I'm sorry... I didn't—"

"Have some pride in your work and do it the right way. Without being asked," Felix said. His tone was low and it was clear without him needing to shout that he would brook no questions or excuses.

Without another word, the driver and Ray—who looked just as sheepish—resumed the task of getting the clock into the house. This time they were careful. Sabine was astonished at the difference. They could have been moving their grandmother herself for all she could tell.

A minute later, the clock landed in an empty space in the dining room, waiting to be unwrapped. Sabine could only hope that beneath the layers of decaying cardboard and clumps of packing tape, her clock was still in one piece.

Felix, meanwhile, had followed everyone in, his hands on his hips, his eyes surveying the scene.

Once the clock was in place and the dolly removed, the

driver produced a receipt, fuzzy from being in his pocket, for Sabine to sign. He spoke very little, merely indicating the space for her signature. Within seconds, he and Ray ducked out, muttering an apology as they scuttled past Felix and out to their truck.

The whole thing took less than three minutes, but Sabine felt like she'd just weathered an overnight storm.

She was worn out. Confused, angry, and exhausted.

But she wasn't about to get a reprieve. Felix was standing in her dining room, his eyes slowly moving over the random collection of boxes and bits of furniture.

Sabine struggled to speak. "Uhhh. Thank you. For setting those two straight. I couldn't believe—"

"No one wants to work anymore. No one ever takes responsibility. They are either trying to con you, or they are just plain lazy. It drives me nuts," he said, his voice laced with irritation.

Sabine couldn't help but feel that some of his frustration was directed at her for allowing those men into her house in the first place. As if she'd even had a choice. They weren't even supposed to be here today.

"Yes. I agree," Sabine said, her hands suddenly feeling strange as they hung at her sides. Something about this man was deeply off-putting. Somehow he made her very aware of her limbs. "Would you like a glass of water?"

The question startled them both—did she even know where her glasses were? Why was she keeping him here longer?

To her surprise, he nodded, saying, "Yes, that would be good. It's hotter outside than I realized."

"Ok..." Sabine mumbled, heading towards the kitchen. "I... uhhh... don't know where..." she fumbled, her anxiety rising as she realized she didn't know where anything was in the pyramid of boxes marked 'kitchen' in her loopy handwriting. "Maybe..." she said, heading towards a box on top of the pile.

To her astonishment, they contained some plastic cups she had thrown in at the last minute when packing her old place. It seemed too good to be true.

"Oh! There we go," she said, relieved to have actually done something right. The stainless steel fridge had a water dispenser, and she gratefully filled two cups, enjoying the slice of cold that flew over her fingertips as she handed one to Felix.

They both sipped, the silence spilling over them even as the cool liquid ran down their throats.

Felix leaned against the countertop while Sabine floated near the fridge, unsure what to do with herself. Within a few seconds, both had stopped sipping their water, and yet the silence lingered, uncomfortable and cloying.

Who was going to bring up the unfortunate incident on the golf cart path first? Or were they just going to pretend it hadn't happened? How or why was Felix standing in her house now? How had he come to be here? Why was she grateful he had showed up exactly when he had? Sabine's mind swirled with questions, but she couldn't find a way to voice any of them.

"I take it... you worked hard... before... retiring?" Sabine asked, her anxiety growing with each stumble.

Felix nodded, his expression unreadable. "Yes. Law and business. Transactions, mostly."

Sabine nodded, unsure what any of that meant. But then again, that's what Colin used to do. He was adept at the business of moving entities around, navigating tricky legalities and loopholes that made men rich and kept the riff-raff out. At the time, she had only vaguely understood what his job was. She never really had a chance to think about it. All she knew was Colin had been very successful at it until...

She tried not to dwell on it. The last year and a half of Colin's life had been plagued by poor health and crumbling business deals. Something she knew hurt him deeply, but that he had never quite shared fully with her. She was convinced, however, it had contributed to his early death.

"Law and business. I've heard of them," she replied, trying to make a small joke that instantly fell flat.

Felix, however, continued, as if he hadn't heard her. "Seems like people knew how to do their jobs back then. Knew what their limits were. Didn't pull nonsense like that," he said, vaguely gesturing in the direction of the grandfather clock.

"Did you work around here or...?"

"Up in Atlanta," Felix replied. "Fischer & Poole."

The title of the firm froze Sabine's blood. She knew that name. She may not have known much of what Colin did, but that name had come up often in their conversations. How Colin had loved working with them and gave them a lot of business over the years. Before things started falling apart.

... until...

Could this man drinking water in my new kitchen be the man who made Colin's last few years on this earth a living hell?

Sabine's face grew hot as she gripped her plastic cup hard enough to feel it click and bend.

"Ah... ok," she croaked, not wishing to talk any further. She had to get this man out of her house. Had to shut the world out. Crawl into a corner and fall asleep. She didn't care if it was on a pile of cardboard. She had to be alone. Now.

Felix seemed to sense the change in the room and abruptly cleared his throat and put the cup down on the counter.

"Well, I should get back. I was just passing by. I hope you don't have any trouble with your clock."

"Yes. Me too," Sabine said curtly, ushering Felix to the front door. She feared that if another minute were to go by with this man in her house, she'd start screaming... or worse.

When they reached the door, Felix turned and said, "About earlier—on the path..." he stopped, his calm demeanor finally showing a hint of uncertainty.

Is he about to apologize? Is he even capable of such a thing? Sabine wondered.

"Yes, I've got it now. New and all," Sabine replied, a prim spin to her words.

Felix shut his mouth and merely nodded, seemingly glad to have the matter behind them.

"See you around," he said, striding out the door that Sabine held open for him.

"Mm-hmm," she replied, closing the door with a decisive thud. She wasn't about to waste any more time on this man.

The instant he was gone, she let out the breath she'd been holding and sank to the floor, her energy spent.

Letting her head fall into her hands, she sighed loudly, a storm of emotions flooding through her.

What am I going to do now?

Chapter 6

Forcing Normalcy

"How are we today?" Sabine crooned, tipping the watering can over the bright blooms. Dahlias and zinnias danced under the falling drops, and Sabine delighted in their showy colors.

"Doing well, I see," she laughed, her eyes scanning the row of flower boxes along the front of her house.

Remarkable, she thought, putting the now empty can on the grass near her. The smell of potting soil and wet leaves surrounded her, making her smile even more.

Amazing what a few days and a hearty dose of gardening can do, she continued. The Florida sun had been kind to her new plants, and the drabness of the front of her house had vanished as the flowers bloomed.

After that disastrous first day, Sabine had thrown herself into unpacking and gardening.

And so far, it had worked. There hadn't been any more forced field trips with Debbie, no unexpected visits from surly delivery drivers—although her phone call with their manager had been less than satisfying. And best of all, no run-ins with either the GGs or Felix.

Truth be told, she had largely kept to herself, only venturing to the common areas when absolutely necessary. Unpacking, sorting, cleaning, and gardening were all a welcome distraction, and in the evenings when her body and brain were foggy and tired, she had her public radio and her books for company.

Though the ache of being alone and starting completely new nagged at the edges of her brain—especially when she found it hard to sleep in the wee hours of the night—throwing herself into making Star Light her home was turning out to be a balm for the soul.

"Right. I'll leave you alone now," she said, being a firm believer in the power of talking to plants. After all, who was she to argue? Plants and flowers had always flourished under her care, and she was cheered to see that, even here in her new home, that hadn't changed.

Putting her gardening tools away and sipping some water, she realized she wasn't ready to go back inside and tackle the last few remaining boxes that stood stacked in the living room. They were just knick-knacks, after all. Little things that were hard to find homes for. Or even things that might be painful to see again.

Gifts from Colin, mostly.

Tokens of their life together.

She'd put these boxes off until the last, and now she knew she couldn't face them. Not today, at least.

"A walk then," she decided, washing her hands and putting a light silk scarf over her hair. She knew she ought to shower but didn't want to ignore the impulse to get moving. It would do her good to get some cardio in before a shower anyway, she reasoned.

Moments later she was through the door, once again

feeling a surge of serotonin from the sight of her flower boxes, glinting in the early afternoon sun.

Breathing the heady scent of banyan trees and spongy, humid air, she headed along the walking path with no destination in mind other than to get some steps in.

Maybe I'll bake something later, she mused, her mind playing over her favorite recipes. *A pie? A turnover? Should I tackle that bread recipe again?*

Lost in her thoughts, she didn't notice the rapid intrusion of dark, menacing clouds from the west. Within seconds, the sky turned from a placid blue to an alarming, all-encompassing gray.

By the time she really noticed it, somewhere along the thick patch of palm trees more than half a mile from her house, it was too late. A crack of thunder split her from her thoughts, followed by great gobs of thick and heavy rain.

"Good lord!" she yelled out, but her voice was instantly swallowed by a sideways gust of wind, which blew rain right into her face. Her filmy scarf was almost lost to the elements before she grabbed it and stuffed it into the pocket of her jeans.

It was too far to run back to her house. Besides, the path was downhill, and largely obscured by a sheet of water.

To Sabine's infinite dismay, her closest shelter was the Comm Center, its yellow lights flashing out at her like a beacon. She ran, careful to keep her footing. An injury would be disastrous. Who would take care of her?

Plowing forward, all rational thought left her. The storm increased in intensity, and her only motivation was to retreat. To stop the slicing sheets of rain from drenching her further.

Blown practically sideways and soaked almost to the

bone, she finally stumbled into the lobby of the Comm Center. A sympathetic receptionist looked up.

"Oh! It's really coming down, isn't it?" the girl said. A flicker of annoyance ran through Sabine. It always irked her when people stated the damn obvious, but something about the young woman's warm smile and welcoming tone warmed Sabine up immediately.

"They've put some towels in the main room. Go ahead and take as many as you like. The storms down here are something else!"

Sabine nodded her thanks and apologies as she left a trail of rainwater behind her like the shoddy train of a dress.

Skin goose-bumping from the blasts of air conditioning, Sabine pushed the ragged strands of hair plastered to her face and headed into the main area of the Comm Center, its oculus window practically black from the storm clouds, the surface studded with rain.

Just as promised, a stack of towels from the swim complex stood neatly piled on one of the side tables, and Sabine eagerly grabbed a few to wipe off her face, and one to drape over her freezing shoulders. Her feet squelched in her shoes. She felt like a drowned rat.

After a few minutes, she had warmed up enough to think straight and moved towards one of the side windows to check on the storm. Florida storms were usually like a child's tantrum: loud, frenetic, and unreasonable, but usually pretty short. She was hoping that was the case here. She wanted to get back to her house and wriggle out of these wet clothes.

The windows told a different story. Outside, the wind made the palm trees bow sideways, like overly supplicant servants. Lightning split the darkness, and the tumble of thunder rattled the walls.

I'm going to be spending a bit more time here, I guess, Sabine thought to herself, hoping to find a hot drink to warm her insides.

At least there aren't a lot of people here today...

As soon as the thought flitted through her brain, she felt the needle of disappointment.

What a colossally wrong assumption to make.

There, sitting in a gaggle in the center of the spacious common room—their usual spot, Sabine suspected—were the GGs. If they'd seen her come in, they hadn't made their observations known. But now they turned almost as one being, looking at her with hungry, beckoning eyes.

This is what it feels like to be fresh meat, Sabine thought, gripping her now sodden towel to her chest. As if this could hide the fact that she was soaked, disheveled, and entirely unprepared to run into them.

Grace crooned across the room. "Oh no! Sabine! Look at you! Don't tell me you got caught in that!"

Isn't it obvious? Sabine remarked silently but smiled wanly instead.

"Yeah, silly me. Out for a walk, and it just snuck up on me."

Grace clucked her tongue, triggering a similar echo in her friends. "This Florida weather certainly is unpredictable. You can never be too sure. I *always* check the weather and never leave the house without a plastic rain bonnet," Grace said sagely, her nose tipping upwards.

"Uh... yes," Sabine said lamely, weighing whether it was better to brave the storm again or stay here in the clutches of the GGs.

Rebecca leaned forward, her coral lipstick slightly crooked and smudged, as if she'd left most of it on the rim of a coffee cup somewhere. "I'm just loving your flowers, Sabine! You have a green thumb!"

Topaz nodded, though it seemed cartoonish rather than genuine. "Oh, for sure. Amaaaaazing." Her head bobbled in agreement, her brown eyes difficult to read behind large designer glasses.

"Well, thanks," Sabine said, trying to separate the filament of good feeling at the compliment from the whisper of warning in thinly veiled mockery.

Will I ever feel comfortable around these women?

"Yes," Grace continued, stepping slightly forward. "You have a lot of hidden talents, don't you? You really have to learn to share them. Star Light is a community, after all."

Sabine felt she was being rebuked, like she hadn't done the assignment. Wasn't she supposed to just *live* here? Did she have to participate too?

"Oh... sure," she replied, "just getting everything set up, you know. Taking a lot longer than I anticipated."

Ginny nodded, her short bob skirting the bottom of her chin. "Oh, I know. I moved here ages ago, and I still have some boxes I've never opened!"

Sabine got the distinct feeling that Ginny was actually trying to have a conversation with her. That she was trying to connect. Ginny's hazel eyes didn't glare or have a hint of sarcasm in them.

Is this real? Can I trust her? Sabine wondered.

Grace cut off further questions.

"So, Sabine, remember when we first met... how you said you'd like to volunteer?"

Sabine opened her mouth to speak, hoping some magical excuse would come to her, fully formed and perfect, when the sound of something resembling a shaking wet dog made everyone turn around to face the entrance to the Comm Center.

Sabine's heart dropped. She heard Grace take in a sharp breath.

It was Felix, looking half drowned, his linen shirt sticking to his skin, the crisp outline of hard muscles clearly visible underneath. His silver hair shone like diamonds as he tossed his head from side to side.

Sabine hated that something deep within her primal side hiccuped for a brief moment, caught up in animal attraction. Her rational mind banished it swiftly, tucking it away into a deep, dark corner of her brain.

No. We will not be attracted to the man who made Colin's life a living hell.

Clearly, for all his time at Star Light, Felix had also failed at mastering the art of looking at the weather before leaving home.

Conflicting thoughts and feelings zipped through Sabine's chest as she tried to keep her face neutral. It's easy enough, given that she kept wiping at it with her towel, despite it becoming bone-dry within moments. Which was more than could be said about other parts of her...

Like a tennis match, the GGs divided their attention between the two sopping creatures, and Sabine felt the air change. A spark of electricity lingering. Her throat tightened. She knew this feeling. It's the feeling right before—

"Don't you two look adorable!" Grace mewed, her fingers playing with the delicate knot of the Versace silken scarf tied elegantly around her neck. "And soaked! Both of you really throw caution to the winds!"

"I think the winds have had their way with them

instead!" Topaz chirped, setting off a twitter of giggles from the group. Sabine and Felix merely looked at each other, an odd mix of unity and derision brewing between them.

"Oh! I have an idea! This is such fun," Grace began, settling her delicate frame on the side of a chair. "Girls, don't you agree?"

Sabine had no idea what they were supposed to agree about since she hadn't announced anything yet, but to her amazement, the GGs nodded enthusiastically, like they'd already held a meeting, introduced the agenda, voted on each item, and set plans in motion via telepathy.

Sabine opened her mouth to question them but then thought better of it and closed it again. No doubt, Grace would reveal herself in time.

"You simply *must* join us!"

Grace stared intently at Sabine and then back to Felix, her pointy tongue skimming her bottom teeth.

After a pause, Sabine ventured, "I... uh... don't know what—"

"The play! Streetcar Named *Desire*!" The last word of the title fell from her thin lips dripping with innuendo. "We need understudies for the leads, and you two would be dreamy for it! Am I right, girls?"

Sabine read Grace's expression intently, her nerves frayed.

What is she going for here? There's no way she wants me to succeed.

There was a hunger in Grace's eyes. An animal need for... something that Sabine suspected was not in her best interest.

Grace shook her head and continued. "Let me explain. The leads—well... sort of the leads—Stella and Stanley— may be out of commission for a performance or two."

She leaned forward conspiratorially, her gaggle following her almost in unison. "The Stella is getting some sort of vein removal, and the Stanley... something to do with his..." she pointed one sharp index nail downward in a gesture Sabine could only interpret as some sort of prostate thing.

"And you need...?" Sabine began.

"*We* need you two to be the understudies! Oh, Felix! You haven't spoken all this time, and you're still dripping wet. Here! Allow me!"

In a flash, Grace took a towel and unfurled it for Felix.

Sabine wasn't sure what had possessed him to stay so long without saying anything, but he took the towel and buried his face in it. When he emerged once more, his face was dry, but his eyes were steely.

At least we seem to agree on one thing: neither of us is into this idea. At all.

"I'm fine," he said finally, his voice low. "Just caught—"

"Like Sabine here! That's why you two are perfect! I can already see the chemistry between you. The sultry New Orleans heat, the smell of beignets in the air..." Grace waxed poetic about the Tennessee Williams classic, and Sabine caught herself exchanging another look with Felix.

Are we... in sync about this? That neither one of us trusts this woman?

"You simply *must* do it! I won't let you rest until you say yes." Grace said, her tone changing in the matter of a split second from convivial to something a tad more cutting.

A stone sunk into Sabine's stomach. She knew that saying no was not an option. Grace was used to having her way, and though it would be painful to submit to her, the thought of not submitting seemed far worse.

Bringing the towel to her face once more, she let most of

her expression hide in the thick fabric, but her eyes crept past Grace's face and back to Felix once more.

There, she could read the same thing she felt: dogged resignation and surrender. Felix knew the consequences too.

"And remember, you promised to be backstage crew anyway, so you'll already be there! This is so perfect!"

Grace clapped her hands together and finally stopped talking. She was waiting for an answer. The chance to celebrate her victory at making two 'volunteers' into conscripts.

"Well? What do we say then?" Grace prodded, a twitch of impatience glinting behind her smile.

Sabine looked at Grace once more and saw her intent written there—Grace wanted to force Sabine into a situation she knew she'd fail. She wanted to make Felix and her look ridiculous. It was all a game to this bored, privileged, petty woman.

And yet, Sabine had no choice but to say...

"Sure! I'd be happy to."

The GGs squealed in unison and then turned to face Felix.

For several seconds, Felix said nothing. Sabine wondered if he was about to defy them when...

"Yes. Okay, then," he replied, his tone even and dry as a desert, belying the tempest raging outside.

"Now, if you'll excuse me, I'm going to get—"

"Coffee's nice and fresh!" Grace called to Felix' retreating back as he headed to the beverage station. "I personally saw to it! Sometimes the staff around here needs reminding."

As she said those last words, her expression fell once

again on Sabine, and somehow Sabine got the impression that she was lumped into that category too. The knot in her stomach grew even larger, but her face locked into a wide, ingenuine smile.

What have I just agreed to?

Chapter 7

Rehearsal Days

"How about my supper, huh? I'm not going to Gal—Galater—galahhhh... what is it again?" Brock Withers called over his shoulder, his forehead crinkled in concentration.

"Galatoire's," Elise, the stage manager replied, a mousy-looking woman with beaded reading glasses tucked onto her bird-like face. She hunched over the script, scribbling notes and following along with the lines as best as she could.

Brock, for his part, looked annoyed. Whether that was because the stage manager—Elsie—had stated the name of the restaurant in Tennessee Williams's script in perfect French dialect or because he simply couldn't remember it correctly was hard to tell.

To Sabine, it hardly mattered since this was about the fifth time Brock had stopped the scene to stumble on this word.

She checked her watch. Again.

How is it possible that only five minutes have elapsed since I last checked? Boy, time moves slowly when people are wretched actors. She winced at the pettiness of the thought but was unable to resist thinking it.

Brock was clumsily handsome—he might have been very good-looking a decade or so ago, but now his once tight jawline was becoming lost in Star Light's abundant buffet dinners even as his stomach strained against his golf shirt. His hair was receding but bore the marks of once being full and possibly brown.

How he had gotten the part of Stanley, Sabine couldn't begin to imagine. Until she looked around the spacious rehearsal hall to see the many posters arranged along the walls. Within seconds, she noticed something: a recurring name over and over:

"Produced by Brock Withers"

"Honorary producer Brock Withers"

"With financial support from Brock...

Sabine looked away.

Ah, the old pay-to-play trick.

She wasn't unfamiliar with the concept. People thought they could buy talent no matter the profession—and especially in theater. But no one said a word. This was the elephant in the room. If they had money, it was generally considered uncouth to point out they had no business to be in 'the business,' but it seemed that even here in Star Light, money had its place amid the hierarchy of community theatricals.

"Let's go back to the top of the scene," Jerrold called, an edge of tension in his voice. "What if you tried saying it really fast? Would that help?" Jerrold's slight fingers played over the patterned scarf tied loosely around his throat, his immaculately pressed linen pants quivering with unreleased energy.

"For sure, Mr. Director," Brock said, rolling his

shoulders and trying to give the impression that he would get this pesky word eventually.

Brock took an exaggerated stance—his approximation of a hard-talking Stanley, complete with sweaty skin and an a-shirt. He poised at the ready, looking at his scene partner.

There was an awkward pause.

"What's my first line?" Trudy asked, her South Jersey accent grating at Sabine's eardrums.

Jerrold made an impatient gesture in the air near Elsie's head, and she dutifully read out, "Oh, Stan!"

Trudy giggled, shaking her head. "Oh, right! Where's my brain?"

Sabine bit her lip to keep herself from making a sarcastic reply.

Were these two really the most seasoned actors at Star Light? Was there no one else? Did people really come to shows knowing they were going to be subjected to this below amateur effort for more than two hours?

The impulse to reply faded, and Sabine let out a small exhale. Looking at her notes, she realized there was nothing new to add to them—she had captured the clunky blocking as best she could and had already memorized most of the scene thanks to Brock and Trudy's repeated attempts to even get it going.

Beside her, Felix sat rigid, his pencil tucked into his script, which was on his lap. It wasn't even open. From his posture, it was clear that Felix was not enjoying the rehearsal in the slightest, and waves of annoyance flitted off him like heat.

At least we can agree that this is horrible, Sabine surmised, although she cautioned herself against ever being sure of what Felix was thinking. The man was a total mystery. Why was he even here? He didn't strike her as the type to do anything he didn't want to do.

Yet, here he was, sitting in a folding chair next to her, suffering through the machinations of Star Light's theatrical stars.

I need to stop assuming things will make sense here. I need to just surrender.

She nodded imperceptibly to herself, willing this to become true. After all, she was in for the long haul now. She had agreed to be the Stella/Trudy understudy, and she was determined to do her best.

Besides, after watching this train wreck for all of twenty minutes, she became convinced she could act circles around this Trudy woman. In fact, she almost welcomed the idea. Just to see the look on GGs faces if she had to go on. She just might surprise them all yet.

Chapter 8

A Visit From the Outside

"Looking great today!" Topaz chimed, her legs wobbling slightly on the oversized adult tricycle she was riding. Sabine looked up from her flowers and raised her trowel in reply. She was glad the sun was obscuring her view because she wasn't sure she'd be able to keep a straight face if she saw Topaz in another light.

Why do we revert back to being children when we retire? she thought, but instantly regretted it. That wasn't fair of her. What was wrong with enjoying your life after so long working and taking care of children and other responsibilities for decades? Why couldn't Topaz rent one of the pastel-colored bikes from the Comm Center and have herself a ride through the grounds if she wanted to?

Topaz nodded and waved before she turned a corner and disappeared. Sabine sat back deep in thought. The greeting from Topaz had seemed genuine—friendly even. Like how adults would greet each other in any other place.

Sabine turned back to her digging, letting her hands cool in the dark potting soil. She knew she should wear gloves—what would Grace say?—but she hated the separation of her skin from the earth. She much preferred to feel the life she was helping to build rather than create a barrier between it. If it meant scrubbing a little longer at the sink, so be it.

As she worked, the smell of freshly tilled earth and warming sun filling her nostrils, she realized something: life was almost—*almost*—starting to feel normal. Or, at least, the type of normal Star Light had to offer.

Raking through the dirt absent-mindedly with her fingers and plucking out any weeds, she tried to reason why she felt even moderately calm. After all, her first days after moving in were chaotic and isolating. Now, however, there seemed to be a thin veneer of tranquility over her days. When she ventured to the Comm, the GGs turned to her with small smiles. It wasn't warmth per se, or anything close to it, but they appeared slightly less brittle and judgmental. At least, that was the way she perceived it. Perhaps they were just laying in wait for their next move to unfold.

So uncharitable! Sabine thought, mentally slapping herself on the wrist. *I must learn to be more open. And trusting. And kind.*

She meditated over the past few weeks, trying to orient her thoughts. Rehearsals were moving along, if not exactly setting the world on fire. Brock and Trudy improved at a glacial pace. And while Grace certainly looked the part of Blanche DuBois, her abilities on stage were wooden and blocky. To Sabine, it was as if the woman managed to lose all her grace and charm the minute she stepped onto the stage.

Then there was Felix.

Lifting her arm to push some wayward hairs that had fallen out of her headscarf, Sabine sat back on her haunches, her brow furrowed in thought. Nearby, she could hear the lazy hum of fat bees circling her newly planted zinnias and hydrangeas.

Felix.

He was an enigma rolled up in a mystery rolled up in... something else she couldn't quite identify.

The night they had laughed themselves silly sparkled in her mind, but it had been so fleeting. A mere moment later, they had said their good nights and headed to their separate houses. Though several rehearsals had gone by and they had managed to behave at all of them—not once interrupting the mighty Brock at his work—he had barely said two words to her since.

Who is this man? Why is he so tricky to pin down? Why does he run hot one minute and freezing cold the next? She shook her head. She couldn't figure him out. It was useless to even try.

Her musing was interrupted by a buzzing in her pocket. Still not used to cell phones, she fumbled to get the darn thing out. She knew she had to have one but never quite embraced being so accessible at all times to all people. Whatever happened to the landline and the cloak of ignorance she could throw over herself if she wanted to avoid someone?

Brushing as much dirt off her fingers as she could, she smiled to see the text that had just arrived:

> On the highway leading to Star Light.
> Should be there in 2 hours. Looking 4ward
> 2 seeing u.

Though she winced slightly at this brand of shorthand, she was glad to know that soon her stepdaughter Hazel would arrive. A welcome distraction, and the first real visitor to her home, which was starting to look and feel like one now that Sabine had poured so much of her time into it.

Standing up slowly and easing the creakiness out of her knees, Sabine decided to call it a day as far as gardening was concerned. She had to shower and prepare dinner if she wanted it to be hot and steaming on the table when Hazel pulled up. Sabine was certain the girl would be hungry.

"See you soon, my lovelies," she called to the flowers that she had just planted. The rest of her garden would just have to wait.

~

"Wowee," Hazel said admiringly, her eyes taking in the house. She closed the door to her sedan slowly as Sabine approached.

"I see it didn't take you long to get the garden going. Or did you cheat and it was already here?" Hazel asked as Sabine wrapped her in a big hug.

"What do you think?" Sabine laughed, pushing the young woman back so she could admire her. Hazel laughed, and Sabine's heart tightened for just a moment as she saw a familiar expression wink back at her. In that moment, she looked just like her dear departed Colin. Sabine swallowed the feeling and put her hand on Hazel's cheek.

"You look tired... but happy," she observed.

Hazel nodded. "You would be right. I've been traveling all over the state for this feature I'm writing. But hey—no one wants to hear someone complain about getting to stay in posh hotels and eat amazing food, so I say nothing. But, yes, I'm tired. Good thing it's my dream job." Hazel's sleek brown bob whisked against her chin, and her signature hazel eyes sparkled in the late afternoon light.

"I have just the remedy," Sabine replied. "A home cooked meal.'

Hazel sighed contentedly. "Just what this weary traveler needs," she said, picking up her small suitcase and following Sabine into the house.

Once they were settled, Sabine served iced tea and homemade sugar cookies. "A little pre-dinner dessert. Because, why not?"

Hazel smiled, a pinch of sadness in her eyes. "Dad always loved to do that. He said life was—"

"Too short to never eat dessert first," Sabine said, joining Hazel in the well-worn—and well-loved—expression.

"He sure did," Sabine said, pushing the cookies towards Hazel. "Eat up."

A moment passed while the two women held their collective grief in the room between them, sharing its weight. Neither wanted to linger there long. Hazel shook her head, dismissing the sadness.

"So, tell me all about this place. I'm fascinated. I may even pitch a feature to my editor about it."

Sabine nibbled a cookie. "What do you mean?"

"Well, these places are like mini worlds; ecosystems all their own. The planning, the amenities, the people, the..."

"Politics. In-crowds. Cliques," Sabine added.

Hazel's cookie stopped halfway to her mouth. "Yeah! That. I bet there are so many weird rules and social groups that wouldn't exist anywhere else."

Sabine, feeling a little uneasy about disclosing how her first few weeks at Star Light had actually gone, hedged, "I suppose so."

Hazel didn't take the bait to change the subject. In fact, quite the opposite. The journalist in her could always smell when someone was hiding something, which Sabine knew only too well.

"Oh come on, Bean," Hazel began, using her familiar nickname. "Spill it. What's this place really like?"

"Oh... I dunno. It's..." Sabine wasn't sure if she wanted to go into it. A part of her knew it might be cathartic—funny, even—to tell Hazel all about the quirks and characters of Star Light, but a strange apprehension drew over her. By speaking these things out loud, would she be forced to realize that they were realities she would have trouble escaping from? Did she want to? Was she finally accepting her life here, or was she ignoring major flaws about it?

She opened her mouth to speak but was saved by the buzzer of her oven.

"Oh! That's the casserole. Be back in a second!" Sabine darted to the kitchen, her steps followed by Hazel's tsking tongue.

"You can't hide for long! I'll get that story out of you!"

"I know!" Sabine replied from the kitchen, pulling the casserole piping hot from the oven. "I know how well trained you are!"

Hazel laughed from the dining room. "Oh, you bet I am! Dad would never let me forget how expensive that degree was!"

Dinner was relaxed and easy-going, as always. They talked of Hazel's travels and experiences in resorts all over the state. Hazel described the unimaginable perks some places offered, along with the more salacious details of her interviews with various general managers, tour guides, and maitre d's. An hour flew by.

"People are too much sometimes!" Hazel shook her head, glittering with amusement. "This one resort up in the panhandle had to ban a woman for bringing her emotional support peacock into her room!"

Sabine laughed, the warm buzz from the rosé Hazel had brought tickling her skin. Her cheeks flushed, and she knew they should probably slow down and not actually finish the whole bottle, which they were very much on track to do. All the same, her hand took up the bottle as if it had a life of its own, refilling their empty glasses.

I have nowhere to go tomorrow, so why not?

"I don't know how some people do it. People can be so..." Sabine said.

"Peopley!" Hazel bellowed, laughing uproariously, her head flung back. Sabine sank into her chair, her belly full and her heart happy. How glad she was to see Hazel—how happy she was to have a guest in her new home. It made this move feel more official somehow. That it had now been christened with the visit of someone whom she loved and who rooted her to her past. A rite of passage she didn't know she needed.

After the laughter fell away, Hazel leaned forward. "Now, let's have it. You haven't told me *a thing* about this place. I'm curious. And you know how I get when I'm *curious*."

Sabine giggled. "Oh, I know. You never let it go."

"Nope. I don't. So, spill. What's this place like? Tell me everything."

A small, cautionary voice in Sabine's head chirruped the reservations she had earlier. However, that was when she was much more sober. She had hesitated telling Hazel about Star Light, but now the wine acted as a great buffer. Sabine took a breath. "Well, my first day here was a doozy..."

With those words, the gates opened, describing the movers and the appearance of Debbie Carruthers, all of which had Hazel in stitches, topping it all with the GGs and all their snide remarks and middle school antics.

"And you're *in* the play?" Hazel asked, her eyes sparkling with curiosity and wine.

"Well, no, not really. I'm in the crew. And I'm understudying Stella..."

"What's that like? Is anyone any good?"

Sabine hesitated, remembering how Felix seemed to know all his lines and how she knew, by instinct, that he would smolder as Stanley were he ever to get the chance to replace the wooden and dreadful Brock in the role.

"Uhh... hard to tell..."

"But?" Hazel prodded.

"No, *but*—there's..."

"There's someone! I can tell! Spill it."

The voice of reason piped up one more time only to be discarded by Sabine's need to share, her need to connect with Hazel—the daughter she had adopted and practically raised.

"Well, there's one. But I'm not sure how to describe him."

Hazel cupped her oval face in her hands, her eagerness apparent. "Try."

"He's aloof. And rude sometimes. And haughty. And... he surprises me sometimes. Well, most times. I never know what he's going to do."

"He's hot, isn't he?" Hazel asked, causing Sabine to almost spit out the sip of wine she had brought to her lips.

Sabine hesitated. Would it be odd for Hazel to hear Sabine admit to such a thing? Colin had not been gone for long, and while Hazel was no wallflower, Sabine wasn't sure if admitting Felix was attractive would cross a line.

But Hazel was persistent. She looked at Sabine expectantly, a devilish smile on her face. Sabine dove in.

"He's... yes. Yes, he is. But there aren't many around here to compare him to; it's not like we're at the top of our game at this stage."

Hazel shrugged. "Don't sell yourselves short. Everyone I saw on the way up here looked amazing. Age is only a construct."

Sabine shrugged. "Easy for you to say."

"Nah, it's true. I bet he's a silver fox. Is he?"

Suddenly, the voice that had cautioned her to not bring up Felix spoke loud and clear:

Don't go there. Think of Colin instead.

"Uhh... yes, I suppose he is," she demurred, wanting to end this conversation quickly but without raising suspicion. It didn't work.

"Are you okay, Bean?" Hazel asked, her curiosity sliding into concern.

"Yes, I am... just think I've had too much to drink. You must be tired. Time for bed, yeah?" Sabine said in a rush, clearing the plates away before anything else could be said.

"Oh sure... I am tired. It'll be good to get some sleep in a room that doesn't come with prepackaged soap."

"For sure," Sabine said, waving away Hazel's attempts to help clean up.

"Go on now. There are towels and anything else you need in your ensuite. Let me know if you... need anything." Sabine giggled, knowing the wine was temporarily ruining her vocabulary.

Hazel paused for a moment, and Sabine worried that she'd start asking questions again—Hazel was a damn good journalist after all—but she simply held out her arms for a hug.

"Night, Bean. Thanks for having me over."

"Anytime. You know that. You are always welcome wherever I am."

Hazel nodded and wandered down the hall to her room. When Sabine heard the click of her door shutting, she sank back into her chair, mildly ashamed of her lack of control.

How could she fawn over Felix when he might have been the cause of Colin's death? How would Hazel feel if she knew that Sabine got butterflies whenever Felix was around? How could she explain that? Hazel had endured Colin's last days as well; she had been a rock when the mourners came and paid their respects. Had helped arrange the funeral and all the paperwork that came after. *So* much paperwork. Sabine could not have done it without Hazel's cool and capable head.

How could she flirt with Colin's enemy?

She pushed her glass of wine away, disgusted at what it had almost done to her.

Who was she? How was she living her life? And how could she get through it with Felix living practically next door?

She left the rest of the dirty dishes where they were. Hazel, she knew, had an early start in the morning, so Sabine figured she had better rest up while she could.

Clicking off the dining room lights, Sabine sighed.

"Who are you, Sabine?" she whispered into the darkness. Only the soft, steady click of the pendulum in her beloved grandfather clock answered her. This time, it provided no comfort.

Chapter 9

Come Hell or HIgh Water

"Come on, come on... heat up, damnit," Sabine said to the sad, overtaxed glue gun that sat on the beat-up work table backstage. Her shoulders ached as she bent over the line of props she'd been making; gluing and fastening various pieces of fake food to dinner plates as part of the poker scenes for the play.

She wasn't sure why she was so anxious. Back here, she was alone. Back here, she was away from the rehearsal onstage, thankfully hidden from Brock's overly loud exclamations and Trudy's fumblings. At least here she could roll her eyes freely.

Though she was supposed to be out front watching Trudy's blundering attempts at remembering her blocking, she had jumped at the request to help with props. It gave her a reason to be away from everything.

And everyone.

Felix was around too, but his earlier efforts to make her laugh or even comment on the action were subdued, nonexistent even. He showed up dutifully but barely said a word or even looked her way. Instead, he buried his nose in his dog-eared script, though Sabine was certain he knew every word. More than Brock did, no doubt.

His presence and his palpable silence made Sabine edgy, and she wanted nothing more than to lose herself in some mindless task. If only the damn glue gun would warm up. The poor thing was definitely on its last legs.

She touched the metal tip again—certain it would be cold.

"Ouch!" she hissed, instantly regretting her boneheaded decision. She put her finger in her mouth, easing the sting of the tiny burn.

"I guess you do still have some life in you after all," she muttered, the irony of what she said in this retirement village not lost on her. She set to work only to be interrupted moments later by the scrape of Elise's sensible shoes and a quiet throat clearing.

"Excuse me, Sabine?" Elise asked, her eyes large behind her spectacles that were now on her face instead of hanging around her neck.

"Yes?" Sabine replied, pulling her finger out of her mouth and feeling sheepish for being seen this way.

"Can you possibly take over for Trudy? There's been a... well. The less said, the better," Elise demurred.

Panic and anxiety flared up deep in Sabine's abdomen, but she didn't want to disappoint Elise. After all, she was one of the few competent people around here. How could she say no to that?

"Uhhh, sure..." Sabine said, unplugging the glue gun and wiping her hands on a raggedy work towel.

Elise let out a small sigh—the stage manager's equivalent of relief. "Great. This way." She led Sabine through the dim hallways of the backstage towards the stage itself. As they walked, they passed by the dressing room, and Sabine heard chaotic, scrambling sounds from the bathroom.

"Oh! I've just exploded with diarrhea!"

Sabine instantly reddened. The voice was unmistakably Trudy's, and, by the smell of things, something terrible had just happened. Sabine was grateful she had not been there to witness it, though she could feel her nose wrinkling in protest. For the briefest of moments, Elise and Sabine caught each other's eyes, and Elise whispered, "Bad reaction to some... diet pills," before they entered the stage area.

"Ah! There she is! Great!" Jerrold said, his voice saccharine sweet. Sabine could tell he was tense but trying to make the best of things. Opening night was dangerously close, and there was still so much to do—not the least of which was to try to find some real talent. Sabine already thought the whole thing was a lost cause, but at least the props would look good.

Except now she was Stella. At least, she would be until Trudy could sort herself and her ruined clothing out.

"Ok! Great! Let's get ready for the top of the scene. Stella is hot. She's fanning herself. Stanley is tense and..." Jerrold waved his hands to begin the scene. Brock, Sabine noticed, was walking low and animal-like—no doubt his idea of sexy and sultry. It just looked like he was suffering from the same problem that Trudy was dealing with in the other room, but Sabine kept her face neutral.

"Try to look like you like him, Sabrina!" Jerrold called.

"It's, uh... Sabine," she said, though she cringed as she did. She hated correcting people.

Jerrold sighed loudly. "Whatever. Let's start the scene!"

Sabine swallowed her pride and focused on Brock.

"What's monkey doings?" he said, his Southern drawl sounding almost like a drunken man.

"Oh... Stan!" Sabine said, wincing at having to pause on her first line. She wasn't sure if she should kiss Brock—that was indicated in the scene, but they had never talked about it. Never even rehearsed it properly, but Brock didn't seem to care or notice. Instead, he grabbed at her waist and planted a wet, cold-lipped kiss somewhere near her mouth and nose. She wanted to gag.

He pushed her back and stared.

"It's your line," he said.

Sabine was thrown. The coldness of his kiss drying on her face made her cringe.

"Oh... right. Uhh... I'm taking Blanche to Gala... gla..."

"Galatoire's!" Brock practically shouted, his smug pride spilling from his lips. Clearly, he was never going to make that mistake again and he was hell-bent on rubbing it in.

"You told me she knew the lines," Jerrold hissed at Elise, his poor attempt at a stage whisper maliciously intended to fail.

Panic and bile rose in Sabine's throat. Hot tears stung the backs of her eyes. She was determined not to lose it in front of these people. She was determined to show them she was better than Trudy. More capable. More *everything*.

"I... do. I just..."

"Never happens to me, but I can understand that it happens to others," Brock mock-whispered in her ear. She couldn't believe what she was hearing. Brock was so clueless! He screwed up his lines every chance he got! What revisionist history was this?

"Start again, sweetheart," Jerrold drawled, his tone sounding like he believed she was incapable of doing just that.

Sabine flashed a quick look to Elise, who looked like she

had the beginnings of an apology on her lips but could do nothing about it.

Sabine cleared her throat, which had gone dry as the Sahara. Brock leaned in to kiss her, but she put up a hand and said her next line as a way of avoiding his cold, clammy lips on hers one more time.

"I'm taking Blanche to Galatoire's for supper, and then... and then..."

The words—so clear in her head only moments before—had dried up. Flown away. Eaten up by anxiety and fear.

Jerrold sighed loudly and pinched the bridge of his nose.

"Keep going," he said through gritted teeth.

Elise fed Sabine her line, and she garbled the rest of the line out in a rush: "and then to a show, because it's your poker night."

She had done it—gotten to the end of the line.

Brock stared at her, his face glib. He didn't open his mouth. Sabine began to doubt what was supposed to happen next. But, for the life of her, she couldn't remember if she had anything more to say.

"I think... I think it's your line..." she nudged.

It was Brock's turn to sigh loudly. "It's not *my* line. You're mistaken," he declared.

Elise piped up. "Actually, it is, Brock. It's: "How about...""

Brock's face blistered red. He knew he had been caught being cocky and yet somehow wanted someone else to take responsibility for it.

Sabine feared that meant her.

"How about my supper, huh? I'm not going to Galatoire's for supper!"

Brock's hand snaked around the top portion of Sabine's arm, and his fingers squeezed. Hard.

Painfully hard.

She drew in a breath and looked into Brock's steely eyes. He wasn't playing Stanley right now. He was playing a guy with a weird axe to grind.

Sabine managed to choke out her next line, "I put you a cold plate on ice."

Brock squeezed even harder and said, "Well, isn't that just dandy?"

"Ow! You're hurting my arm!" Sabine cried out, unable to take the vise-like grip any longer.

Brock jumped back like he'd been stung.

"That's the blocking, babe. That's what we have to do. That's what Trudy agreed to. She's a champ about it."

His words came out in a classic frat-boy-suddenly-in-trouble rush. If he talked long and fast enough, he'd get out of taking any blame. Sabine was incensed. Surely now someone would jump in to rescue her? She looked at Elise, who had buried her face in the script. Jerrold was turning as red as Brock.

Felix was nowhere to be seen.

"Sarah, this is ridiculous," Jerrold said. "You can't be a diva right now. You are the understudy. Do you understand that? Do you understand what that means? We don't need extra drama here." His condescension was insufferable, punctuated by Brock's vociferous nodding.

"It's Sabine," she retorted, anger cascading up through her. "And I don't care what my job is, it's certainly not to get roughed up by a guy that can't remember his own lines!"

The two men almost choked in response, and Elise's head snapped up, her glasses chain whipping back towards her ears.

"I can't work like this!" Brock protested, immediately appealing to his enabler and fellow bully, Jerrold. Naturally, the director doubled down and locked eyes with Sabine.

"Brock's right. We can't work like this. It's clear you don't have what it takes—"

Sabine cut him off.

"I don't think community theatre directors are in any position to tell me what I can and cannot do with my body. Find yourself a new understudy. I'm done!"

And with that, she stormed out, tears lashing at the back of her eyes. She refused to let them show before she could leave the room. She refused to give them that satisfaction.

As fast as she could without running, she left the rehearsal room, her steps quick and sure despite the melon-sized sob lodged in her throat.

Just get out. Just get home. Just get away from these bullies, she told herself, repeating it over and over again as she left the theatre and headed up the walking path to her house.

The night air was claustrophobic, like she'd stuck her head inside a sweater on a summer day. The air was moist, dense.

As soon as she was out of sight from the theatre, she opened her mouth and sobbed loudly, ugly-crying at its worst. How could those grown men treat her so harshly? How did they get away with it? Why did Elise not come to her aid? Why were they such awful, callous, cruel people? This was a retirement village, not boot camp.

At least—that was what the advertisement promised.

That's what Sabine thought she was doing here. Or, what she had been striving to do after those first few rocky weeks, but had she been deluding herself?

She ran-walked to her house, the night so close and clammy that sweat broke out along her skin and hairline. Her feet took the lead since her vision was almost completely obscured from crying. She just wanted to be home. To be in her own space. To be alone with her thoughts.

Suddenly, a crack of thunder jarred her from her misery, and the heavens opened. "Oh no, no, no," she moaned as slashes of rain cut loose.

Within the space of ten feet, she was soaked, her feet sploshing as they carried her forward.

Her hair was glued to her cheeks, and her tears mixed with the rain, fresh water and salt.

A few minutes later, drenched and miserable, she stumbled through her front door, eager to shed all her clothes, dive into a warm bath, and down a bottle of wine. She had to think about what she would do next. Where she could go. She couldn't stay here, could she? Could she really make a life here? Was she fooling herself to think she could call these shallow monsters her neighbors? They certainly could never be friends.

Tossing her sodden purse onto the foyer table and shucking her sopping shoes, she started toward the bathroom, pulling up short at loud knocking on her front door.

She froze, hoping whoever it was hadn't seen her enter just moments before. Maybe if she just remained still enough, they would go away. Leave her utterly alone.

Ten seconds passed. Sabine barely breathed.

Then... another knock. More insistent this time.

She couldn't put them off. She knew that. With a sinking heart, she padded towards the entryway, leaving droplets of water in her wake.

Opening the door, the wind sluiced past her, the rain practically going sideways.

She gasped at the sight of her visitor. He was soaked to the skin, his short-sleeved shirt clinging to chiseled muscles and smooth skin.

"Felix! What are you doing here?" she asked, her hand gripping her doorframe.

"I... had to make sure you were okay. Are you?"

A gust of wind took her words away. Not that she had any.

What was Felix Crenshaw doing on her doorstep?

Chapter 10

Flustered and Flabbergasted...

"I ... come in. You should come in," Sabine said, her words barely audible above the wind and rain.

Splashes of water speckled her threshold, and the picture frames and knickknacks on the side table where she kept keys and stray pieces of mail rattled and shook.

Felix nodded, taking a step inside. Sabine closed the door behind him, instantly hushing the din.

He looked at her, concern lacing his face. A stray lock of wet hair spliced one of his eyes in half, but his gaze didn't waver. Beneath his sculpted beard, his jaw was tight and set. Sabine did her best to look away from the dripping shirt clinging to his drenched skin.

The muscles under the thin fabric were taut and rippled. The muscles of someone who took care of himself. The muscles of a seemingly much younger man.

"Seems like we keep meeting like this," Felix said, his voice low. "Rainstorms."

For a moment, Sabine said nothing. She wasn't actually listening to him. Rather, she had become fascinated by how his mouth formed words, the alluring shape of his lips and teeth, and the tiny flicker of the pink of his tongue.

The moment spun out far too long. With a jolt, she realized he was waiting for her to speak.

"Oh! Where are my manners? Here!" Sabine darted to the linen closet and produced two thick towels, one for each of them.

He took his gratefully, burying his face in it as she did the same. She knew she should mop up the mess in the foyer, but something about Felix's mood stopped her. That and the fact that he was standing there in the first place. What was he doing here, exactly?

The towel did its job, and within moments, she felt slightly more human. Felix, she noticed, had unbuttoned some of his shirt to better dry himself. She stared at a point on the floor near his feet.

Finally, she plucked up enough courage and opened her mouth to speak. Felix did the same.

"I suppose you're wondering why I'm here..." he began.

"I was, actually."

"I heard the way they spoke to you back there. They had no right."

The stinging memory of what had happened at the theatre burned over to Sabine, hot and fresh. In the confusion of Felix's arrival, she had almost forgotten about it.

"Uhh... yeah. It was—"

"They are talentless hacks and should not have said those things. I was coming back from a fitting when I heard the tail end of it. I tried to get to you before you left, but..."

Sabine looked at him, decisively this time. "Before I left, yes. I'm not proud of that."

Felix kept his eyes on hers.

"Nothing to apologize for. You had every right to leave. You have been doing them a favor. That Brock is a poison. Throwing his money around with no talent to back it up."

Sabine nodded. "It should be you up there."

Felix made a murmuring sound. "Maybe. But I don't finance the season. And besides, they don't want real talent up there. Then where would they be?"

Sabine shrugged, feeling the pull of her wet clothes against her shoulders. "Not sure."

"Anyway, I'm just here to check up on you. Make sure you're okay. I was going to call, but I realized I don't have your number. So... you okay?"

Sabine met his eyes again and found a genuine warmth there. When had she last seen or felt that? From Hazel? From Colin before she lost him?

Her cheeks flushed, and her body grew warm. She took a few controlled breaths, trying to slow down the avalanche of competing thoughts in her head. Her body and brain were locked tight in an epic battle. She didn't ask to feel this way—she hated that her body seemed to betray her rational, logical thoughts.

Or were they?

"Yes. I'll be okay. Thank you. It was kind of you to come by."

He looked at her for a long moment before nodding to himself and shifting his weight. "Well, okay then. I... uh... here's your towel. I should get going."

He held his hand out, returning the damp towel. She reached out to take it, their hands grazing in the exchange. A bolt zinged through her, and a sharp intake of breath flooded her lungs. Catching his eye, she saw that he felt something too. His eyes lit up with surprise and something else.

Desire.

Instead of pulling her hand away, she remained there, the grazing of their skin deepening. They were unequivocally touching each other's hand, feeling the rough parts and smooth, the wrinkles and the life that had lived through those fingers. A lifetime of memories and sensations.

Her body drew forward, almost of its own propulsion. He did the same. Like magnets drawing close. No power could stop them. Even if she wanted to. Even if her higher brain could not shake the doubts of who this man was and who he might have been to her former partner.

None of it mattered just then. None of that made any sense. The only thing that mattered was their bodies drawing closer together. Shrinking the space between them.

Their hands skidded upwards, hers traveling the distance from hand to wrist to elbow to shoulder. She felt muscles, sinew, fabric, and skin. He must have felt the same, her body heat drying the thin blouse she wore.

Within seconds, their mouths were mere inches apart. His breath scalding her neck, his eyes searching.

Before she could stop herself, she leaned in and closed the gap entirely.

Their lips met. Electric shocks cascaded down her throat, through her chest, and down each leg to the floor below. A delicious sap.

His hand landed on the small of her back, drawing her closer.

The kiss deepened. The damp towel fell to the floor, soaking up the raindrops that had settled there.

Chapter 11

Sweet, Sweet Connection

"Is this..." Felix murmured, mid-kiss. Two tugging forces of energy battled through Sabine; one drove them both into whatever was happening now, and the other screamed a single word.

Caution!

She needed to take a breather. At least a tiny one. She pulled back from his embrace, her breath shallow and rapid.

"Is this... what?" she asked, brushing her damp hair back from her flushed cheeks and looking up into his face. "Are you okay?" Each word came punctuated by exhalation.

Felix looked at her, his eyes filled with hunger and something else—care? Concern? An awareness of... what, exactly?

"I'm fine. More than fine. I just... I haven't done this in a while."

Something new bloomed inside Sabine. A mixture of surprise and delight, warmth and longing.

This gorgeous man hasn't had this kind of attention in a while? Really?

It only made her want him more.

"Neither have I," she replied, her words barely above a whisper. "But I'm okay... if you are."

Felix didn't use words to respond but merely smiled slyly and started kissing her again. In an instant, Sabine knew the cautionary voice would have to take a backseat. It was no longer welcome.

For now, anyway.

Felix may have had a dry spell, but he wasn't exactly out of practice. His mouth and tongue found hers and kissed her deep and long, giving and receiving in equal measure. Sabine leaned into him, their damp, rain-soaked chests coming together, rapidly drying the fabric.

His hands found her hair, fingers snaking through it, pulling lightly, just enough to make her scalp tingle but not enough to cause pain. She gasped through the kissing, pleasure zipping along her entire body.

"Mmmm, thought you might like that," Felix whispered. Though she couldn't see it, she could feel Felix wink as he spoke, their shyness melting into boldness.

"Mmm-hmmm," she replied, her fingers fanning out over the broad musculature of his back, feeling how the ridges and bumps moved as he pressed his body closer to hers.

As they kissed, their feet did a dance of their own, shedding shoes and kicking them out of the way. The pile of wet towels and sopping footwear joined the puddles on the floor.

"This way," Sabine whispered, laying her hands on Felix's rippled chest to guide him towards the living room.

He broke away from her touch, giving her a naughty grin.

"Here?" he asked, pointing to her gigantic sofa,

festooned with a riot of throw pillows of various patterns, shades, and shapes. Sabine loved a good, comfy couch. A place to read and settle at the end of the day.

Or, to engage in other, spicier activities...

"That's the place," she replied, enjoying the purr of her voice. A voice she had not heard from her throat in such a long time.

Felix took her hand and pulled her close to him as they stood near the couch. He reached up and stroked her cheek, looking with deep longing at her eyes, her cheeks, her lips. He bent towards her, letting kisses graze her throat, the valley at the base of her neck.

Sabine let her head fall back and shut her eyes so she could savor his attention, reveling in his kisses. Her fingertips traced over the tops of his shoulders, down his arms.

Then, his fingers found the buttons of her shirt. First one, then two, the fabric falling open, the soft breeze of the air conditioning (set at a comfortable 72 degrees) gently brushed her skin. She was glad she had worn her pretty lavender bra. What luck, considering most of her undergarments were of the utilitarian variety and nothing quite as fetching.

Felix moaned his approval as his mouth traveled from her neck across her shoulders, then down and down and down...

"Oh," Sabine groaned as he gently moved the lacy fabric downwards, exposing the top of her breast. Just under the lace edge, she felt her nipples grow hard. She had forgotten this sensation and delighted in its return.

"Beautiful," Felix murmured as he reached up her back and deftly snapped the clasp with two fingers. His other hand caught the bra and tossed it lightly to the side.

Even in her distracted state, Sabine had to marvel at his skill.

But she didn't have time to think further. His mouth found her left nipple, a flashing warmth and shocks of pleasure melting through her. He cupped her breast as he licked, teasing and caressing her. Reaching up, she took hold of her other breast, eager that both should feel attention. Felix gave a grunt of pleasure.

Then, in a mad dash of movement, she pushed him back, a scalding need to share these feelings. She pulled at his shirt, yanking it over his head to land somewhere on the floor. Her eyes drank in his tanned and toned body, the hints at aging only enhancing him. Making him somehow *more* attractive.

Like an optical illusion, she thought, smiling inwardly. She'd always loved optical illusions.

"Like what you see?" he asked, his eyes flashing.

"I do," she replied, her hands already pulling him back to her. She noticed the unmistakable bulge in his linen pants; another sign that he was most definitely a catch.

Felix paused once more.

"If that's so, we should appreciate the whole picture," he said, his voice a raspy, voracious growl. In a second, he whipped off his remaining clothes, his speed and flexibility alarming and magical all at once.

Sabine practically squealed with delight, cupping her hands over her mouth.

"How did you do that?!" she exclaimed. Everything about this man was a surprise.

"Not sure. No doubt I'll pay for it later," Felix said, the mischief of that night at rehearsal filling him once more. This was the Felix Sabine had become attracted to. Now standing naked and smiling in her living room. In the middle of a rainstorm.

Stranger things must have happened...

Just not to me.

Until now.

"Your. Turn," Felix commanded.

If Sabine had any reservations, they didn't hold her back. Though not as quick and agile as Felix, she stepped out of her now mostly dry capri pants and underwear, her skin hot and tingly, receptive to every motion and touch.

Felix's eyes looked at her long and appraisingly, his desire evident in his face and in his manhood. The sight of him throbbing before her made Sabine grow wet between her legs. Something she had not felt in so long that she gasped again.

"You okay?" Felix asked, some of his desire melting.

Sabine didn't answer with words but merely pulled him to her, unable to make her body wait any longer. Their skin connected, hot and rapid, sending ripples of pleasure throughout them both. Their hands went to work, exploring, caressing, kneading, and stroking, each one mapping out the hills and valleys of the other. The rough parts and the smooth. From the wrinkles to those parts seemingly untouched by time.

Sabine felt like a twenty-something again, her body racing before her head, her impulses in the driver's seat, her skin aching for every touch.

Their mouths connected, the kisses deeper and more frenetic, as if a hunger neither one could contain had been unleashed. Sabine no longer thought in words or cogent phrases but merely in sensation, need, and want. Base instincts that pushed her further and further towards...

Felix took her shoulders and gently sat her down on the

couch. He pulled back, his mouth open as he took deep, controlling breaths. His cheeks were flushed, and his hairline stood dotted with sweat, his chest had a sheen over it so that he practically glowed.

Their eyes locked, he placed a hand between her breasts and pushed her back into the soft embrace of the pillows, a playful smile on his lips. When the couch had fully enveloped her weight, he removed his hands and gently and slowly—oh, so slowly—opened her knees as he sank down between them.

Sabine's eyes opened wide as she comprehended his intentions.

Was he going to... go there? On me?

She couldn't remember the last time she had felt someone's warmth down there, how long it had been since she'd—

"Ah!" A moan flew out of her as all thoughts abandoned her at once. His mouth found her, licking her so gently, each tiny movement of his tongue sending flames through her body and brain. She closed her eyes, the pleasure sinking into her like a warm bath.

His hands moved upwards, his fingers expertly taking her nipples and touching them in tandem with his tongue, which began to probe deeper and deeper, faster and faster.

Any semblance of logic or rational thought completely abandoned her. All thoughts now came in the form of sensation and color like riots of fireworks in her head.

Her hips started to rock to his rhythm, her body and his tongue in complete sync. Sabine bit her lip as the movements increased in speed and intensity.

Opening her legs even wider, she squeezed her eyes shut and surrendered to him completely. All the colors in her head suddenly shattered to pitch black.

"Oh, Felix!" she screamed as she came, her body pitching upwards in an electric arc. Her toes pushed her whole body upwards, her hips leaving the soft couch for a moment before sinking back down.

Oblivion descended on her for a few blissful moments before the blackness in her head started to populate once more with colors—muted at first but then rising in saturation and vividness.

She opened her eyes. Felix sat back, his face shining, his hair mussed. He looked pretty damn pleased with himself, and Sabine couldn't blame him. At all.

She licked her lips, which had gone dry. She murmured, "It's been a while for me too."

"And?" he asked, arching one eyebrow.

"And," she replied, laughing slightly, "that was one hell of a way to come back!"

He smiled, one side of his mouth curling higher than the other. He looked devilish and absolutely irresistible.

"But we're not done yet," she said, crooking her finger and beckoning him forward. He obliged, though she marked the slight twinge in his face as she heard his knees creak.

"Come here, you can't stay on the floor," she urged, pulling him onto the couch with her.

They settled into the mass of pillows. The feel of his skin once again sent ripples through her. Sabine gasped at his hardness on her thigh. Before she knew what she was doing, she reached down and took hold of it, stroking it slowly.

Now it was Felix's turn to close his eyes in appreciation. He groaned softly, one tooth biting his bottom lip. Sabine kissed him, causing his eyes to flutter open in surprise. They basked in looking at each other, their connection magnetic.

She continued to stroke him, her hand moving up and

down, faster and faster. He was smooth and hard, his long shaft utterly perfect. She had never seen one quite like it.

Felix was impressive in all the ways he should be.

Then, a deep, visceral longing overtook Sabine. They needed to be closer. She needed to embrace this man, fully and completely. She couldn't wait any longer.

"Get inside me," she directed, surprising them both with her ardor. It came out as a growl, a directive that brooked no dispute.

Felix looked at her with questions in his eyes. Still the gentleman.

"I *need* you," Sabine said. "I just…"

He didn't let her finish the sentence, pushing himself up on the couch until he was above her, his silver hair falling into his eyes, shading them from the living room lamps.

She opened her legs and looked at him imploringly, her skin resonating heat and want.

Their eyes locked in a silent conversation of connection that could never be translated.

Slowly and with great care, Felix lowered his body down, the muscles of his arms flexing and rippling. Sabine wove her hands around his back, tickling at his shoulders, his neck, his hair.

Then, with a sharp inhale, Felix entered her, their breaths catching in unison. For a split second, Sabine lost all grasp on any language but the pulsing movement into her body.

How long had it been since she'd felt this free? This open? This connected to another person?

For a moment, Felix didn't move. He simply stayed within her, their eyes transmitting the secrets of their selves to the other. A tenuous, gorgeous connection.

Then, by some cue that only the two of them could

fathom, they began to move in rhythm. Felix's body pulled from Sabine, and she pushed forward. Then again. And again. Delicious friction growing faster and more intense with each push and pull.

Sabine's fingers laced and twirled over the Felix's back, raking red lines on his skin. In return his hands locked into her hair, his breathing becoming faster and faster as he nuzzled into her neck.

The pillows around them bounced and fell to the floor, adding to the pile of damp clothing. Outside, the wind continued to howl and the rain slanted sideways, as if in concert with the delicious sinful chaos taking place in Sabine's living room.

"Oh... you feel... amazing," Felix uttered, his breath hot on her neck. Sabine couldn't reply but merely groaned in agreement, her eyes squeezed shut. Her legs wrapped around his hips as they continued to move together and break apart faster and faster. She lost all sense of time and place and physics and...

Suddenly, Felix's body went rigid as his teeth clenched and a loud exclamation of utter pleasure bubbled from his loins to his mouth. Sabine echoed his feelings and moaned back. Their bodies slick with sweat.

Momentarily suspended, the only sound in the room for a brief second was the ticking of the grandfather clock. A second later, Felix exhaled loudly and sank his body into Sabine's, causing more pillows to fall to the floor.

They lay still, sticky and happy, their pulses slowing as the rain continued outside.

Sabine's fingers stilled on Felix's back and came to rest there, savoring the post-coital glow.

Wind rattled over the roof, bringing Sabine back into

the present. Vaguely, she became aware of what had just happened, how it had happened, and....

What was next?

She shoved that question away, desiring only to live in this moment, this point of time.

Closing her eyes, she concentrated on Felix's breathing as it slowed, matching her own.

Chapter 12

Sweet and Sour Awkwardness

"Ow! Ow, ow, ow!" Sabine yelped herself awake, her calf locked in a brutal charley horse that had rudely yanked her from a deep sleep.

Her back arched as she breathed noisily through her teeth, trying her best not to thrash too much on her pillow.

A more rational voice somewhere in the back of her head admonished her for not drinking enough water—she knew damn well this is why she was getting a leg cramp, but thinking this didn't help. There was simply no way around a leg cramp but through. And breathing and relaxing, which seemed damn near impossible.

Gritting her teeth, the pain slowly subsided, leaving nothing but a dull ache. She settled back into her sheets and realized that she was naked. Completely naked.

And that she was not alone.

"Are you okay?" came a deep voice, and Sabine nearly had another leg cramp.

Felix.

Felix Crenshaw was in her bed. Because of course he was. She hadn't been drunk, drugged, or delusional the night before. She had merely succumbed to her most carnal desires.

And they had been carnal, indeed. She couldn't remember the last time she had felt such things.

Or done such things.

"Uhhh, yes," she stammered, pulling a sheet over her chest and tucking it beneath her bottom. It was odd that she suddenly felt so self-conscious. Hypocritical even, given all the things they had done together. But that was last night—when the world was storming outside.

Inside too, if she was being honest.

But, here, in the bright gooey sunshine of the day, things were much, much different.

Felix leaned up on one elbow, his silver hair tousled and matted on one side. His eyes looked creased, and he moved stiffly.

Was he feeling silly too? Regretful? Ashamed?

Sabine couldn't read him, so she merely looked up towards her ceiling instead, charting the ribbons of morning light that danced through the half-closed blinds. It occurred to her now that she hadn't shut up the house properly, probably had not shut off the outside lights or even cleaned up the soggy mess in the foyer.

The last thing she remembered was stumbling away from the couch in a hurried heap of legs and arms, the two of them eager to lie somewhere a bit more comfortable. The couch was fine for a few things, but sleeping overnight was not one of them.

"Just a wicked leg cramp, is all," Sabine said, gingerly wiggling her toes and rotating her ankle to work out the sore muscles.

Felix mumbled back. "Mmm-hmm. I know all about those."

She thought she ought to feel kinship with him at that moment, a sort of bonding over the aches and pains of getting older. All the little things she rarely felt except when waking up each morning. That treacherous time when her body took a bit longer to get going. But she wasn't ancient. And neither was he. Last night was a testament to that.

Instead of feeling close to him, a feeling of isolation swept over her, coupled with an intense awkwardness. Felix must have sensed it because he sat up, rotated his shoulders, and moved his neck from side to side to work out some kinks. Her eyes drifted to his bare back, unable to resist the muscles undulating and arching on his fine frame. Besides, it was easier to admire his back than to face him full on.

"Good morning," Sabine said, trying to get a mulligan on the day. Trying to snatch a little of last night's magic back —if only to feel less awkward.

"Morning," Felix said, grunting as he stretched. She heard him hiss through his teeth.

"You okay?" It was her turn to ask.

"Yes," he said, though his tone was strained. "Just... might have... overdone some things."

If Sabine were feeling braver, this might have drawn her to him. It might have knocked away these anxious moments and allowed them to grow close once more, but instead she felt even more isolated, more marooned.

And old.

She felt old.

"I'll just—" she began but quickly stopped when Felix stood up abruptly and padded to her ensuite bathroom and shut the door. A moment later she heard water running and the toilet flushing.

Quickly, she got up and put on her blandest pajamas. It took some finding, however. Her drawer was filled with sleepwear designed for a single lady of the over-65 set. Finally, she settled on something sensible—a sand-colored set with demure bows at the wrists. Throwing a bathrobe on over that, she went to the kitchen to prepare coffee.

The evidence in the living room and the foyer might have looked enticing last night, but here in the light of the morning, it looked something akin to a crime scene. Sodden, crumpled clothes lay on the floor, shoes thrown willy-nilly, and the couch cushions littered the rug.

Sabine bustled past, eager to make a strong pot of her best beans. She was going to need them today.

A moment later, Felix appeared, clutching a small hand towel over his middle. He seemed subdued, but even so, his rugged features and glinting eyes rendered him devilishly handsome. Sabine marveled at how last night had even come to be. And what it all meant now.

"I'm making coffee," Sabine said and then watched with horror as Felix bent down to retrieve his clothes. "Oh!" she exclaimed. "They're damp! You can't wear those!"

Reaching out to take them from him, Felix stepped back, quickly throwing on his linen shirt. A moment later, he had put on his lightweight trousers—still damp and splotchy in places and dry in others.

"Let me throw those in the dryer real quick! You shouldn't wear those like that!" Sabine could tell from Felix's pinched expression and shrunken shoulders that the feeling of the cold clothes was deeply unpleasant but he wasn't giving in.

"Nah. It's ok. I'm fine. Have to get back," Felix said, though what he had to get back to wasn't exactly clear, nor did he elaborate further.

"Let me at least make you some breakfast. I make a mean corned beef hash..." Sabine said, her eyes trying to connect with his but somehow failing and landing on a spot near his chin instead.

Why did she feel so foolish around him? So unworthy? She'd slept with people before—albeit it had been a while. Had she always been this awkward the day after?

I thought that when you got older you were supposed to be better at these sorts of things. Why do I seem to be worse?

Felix waved a hand, already turning his back on her. "No, thanks. Really. I'm okay. I'll..."

He headed to her front door. Sabine trailed behind, feeling like a 1950s housewife, sending her emotionally distant husband off to the office so she could spend the day buying groceries and making ambrosia.

Felix reached the door and pulled it open. Warm, citrus-laced air meandered in, a mix of humidity and freshness from the storm the night before.

Sabine stopped, unwilling to fight for his attention anymore.

Before moving any further, Felix stopped, apparently sensing her pursuit was over.

Or had his manners caught up with him at last?

"Thanks... for last night," he said, a curiously guarded expression on his face. "I had fun. And I... hope things are better for you with the theatre group. Or, at least, they leave you alone from now on. I can see to that."

"Umm, ok," she replied, unable to unpack this odd, stifled little speech.

A moment zinged between them—a slight change in the chemistry of the air—a hint of what connected them so fiercely only hours before. Sabine's mind tried to grasp at it, if only to assure herself that last night wasn't some crazy dream.

It vanished just as quickly, snuffed out by a distant bird

call and a whipping breeze that rattled the door. Felix looked at her once more. "Until... soon," he said and then briskly walked through the door, closing it behind him.

Sabine stood motionless, her feet like cement.

The man who had just left was not the man of the night before. Which Felix was he right now? Which one would she meet in the Comm Center? Worse still, which Felix would she have to deal with going forward? And how could she do it?

How could she deal with anyone at Star Light, really? Her reputation at the theatre was now in tatters, and if word got back to the GGs, what would that mean?

As of this moment, the one person she had briefly connected to had behaved like some kind of automaton.

With heavy steps, she made her way to the kitchen, the smell of fresh-brewed coffee the only good thing about the morning.

Pouring some into her favorite chunky ceramic mug, she sat at her kitchen table, her eyes glazing over the bright splashes of color that made her flower garden pop in the morning sunshine.

She should get out there.

Slough off last night, and tackle the back garden, but her limbs had locked. Even lifting the mug to and from her lips was a trial. The steam whirled and wafted over her face. She breathed in the comforting aroma, but it didn't do much to lift her spirits.

The world outside felt like a prison. Full to bursting with people who didn't want to see her, and she was sure she didn't want to see herself.

What was she going to do now?

Chapter 13

Let's Run Some Tests

"Okay, Mr. Crenshaw, if you can take a seat for me, that would be great," the medical assistant said, her voice chipper. She turned away from him, busy with logging into the computer system. Her long, brown braid swung down past her lower back, bright against her blue scrubs.

Felix leaned slightly forward as he took the seat nearest the exam room door. He tried to avoid the exam table as much as possible. According to her name tag, the assistant's name was Heidi. Having finished her typing, Heidi looked up and frowned slightly. Apparently, the seat he had chosen was less than ideal.

Well, I'm not moving, Felix thought grumpily. He hated going to the doctor's for any occasion. Today was no different.

"Oh, okay..." Heidi said, forcing her smile back into place. With some effort, she pulled an apparatus containing a digital thermometer, blood pressure cuff, and other medical instruments across the examining room towards him. He could tell she was trying to work out how she would run her tests and also update the chart at the same time. He smiled inwardly at his small act of passive aggressiveness.

Still, it did nothing to stop the proceedings.

"Okay, Mr. Crenshaw, let's take your temperature and blood pressure. I'll ask you some questions, and then Dr. Ellers will be right in. Does that sound okay?"

"Do I have a choice?" Felix grumbled, shooting her a look.

She smiled weakly but held firm.

"No, I suppose you don't. Not if you want to get this over with."

He nodded, appreciating her candor. It reminded him of the old days, when people finally got down to the bottom line.

"Alright." He nodded, clapping his hands on his knees with a tight smile. "Let's get on with it."

"Sure thing," Heidi replied, moving quickly. He got the impression she wanted to get this over with as well.

Just another grumpy old codger in for a checkup. How does she do this day after day?

Heidi strapped the blood pressure cuff to his arm and started the machine. He was grateful for the chance to stay quiet and still. His mind immediately wandered.

But why am I so grumpy? There's no reason for it. None at all. Especially considering...

"Oh, huh." Heidi frowned at the machine. "There was a little spike there. Not sure what that's about. Let's re-run this, okay?" She seemed frustrated at the equipment, but Felix knew the real reason the reading was off.

Sabine.

He had just recalled, with startling and lurid detail, the events of last night. The dampness of Sabine's hair, the soft plumpness of her lips, the curve of her waist, sliding out to the bloom of her hips…

"Let's give that a rest for a minute so we can get a better reading. Coming in right away must be messing with your pressures. Let's give you a chance to relax a bit."

Felix nodded, smirking inwardly at his small act of medical rebellion.

"Sounds good," he said, rolling down his shirt sleeve.

"All right. Let's just get these questions out of the way then," Heidi continued, her feet pushing her across the room on a three-legged wheeled stool towards the computer. She looked into the checklist that gleamed down at her.

"Mmm-hmm," Felix replied, aware that the temporary glow of thinking about Sabine's soft skin and musky perfume was fading away, about to be lost to a litany of tiresome questions.

"Any new medications?" Heidi began.

"No."

"How's your sleep?"

"Fine. Not great but fine," Felix replied, annoyed at the fact that at least once a night he had to visit the little boy's room.

"Mmm, okay," Heidi said, tapping something into the form. "What about diet? Any concerns there?"

"Only that I can't have coffee after two pm," Felix replied.

"I understand that," Heidi said, in a show of chummy familiarity. "Anything else you want to tell me? Anything to report?"

Felix shrugged. Nothing was bothering him. Nothing was wrong. He only did this once a year to keep the grim reaper at bay. All he wanted was to have this appointment over and done with. He wasn't about to volunteer a damn thing.

And yet... didn't something unusual happen just last night?

A flutter thrummed between his ribs. The same feeling that had coursed through only moments before when the blood pressure cuff was trying to get a reading. Being with Sabine last night energized him, made his stomach contract in a pleasant way, made him catch his breath a bit. Made his groin...

"Mr. Crenshaw?" Heidi prodded, her head cocked to the side as if concerned. "Anything else you want to tell me?"

He grunted, angry at himself for getting caught thinking dirty thoughts in front of this young woman. She was practically a child!

"Uh, no. Nothing," he growled.

"Okay, then. I'll just go and get Dr. Ellers then. Not much longer now," Heidi replied, her relief at leaving the room evident. "You stay put."

What else would I do? Felix thought, but the ire didn't last long. Mostly, he felt foolish. Losing himself to dirty thoughts at a doctor's appointment. What happened last night was a fluke, a passing flight of fancy. Possibly a gross error of judgment. Nothing more.

Sabine was a far cry from the women who had previously been in Felix's life. He had always connected with sleek women of commerce. Women with sculpted hair, designer clothes, and nails that could scratch steel. Women who worked in powerhouse positions like he had. Women with tough skin and even tougher hearts.

They were fun to sleep with, but there was nothing soft about them.

That's what made Sabine such an outlier.

What am I doing sleeping with a woman who owns an NPR tote bag? Someone who probably reads horoscopes in papers like the Wall Street Journal. We have nothing in common. Her house smelled like a scented candle.

Felix shrugged off the thoughts. It had been a one night stand. Nothing more. Now, he'd just have to figure out how to shrug her off kindly—but clearly—when they next bumped into each other.

A soft knock interrupted any further thoughts.

"Good morning, Mr. Crenshaw," Dr. Ellers said, stepping inside, closing the door, and deftly taking a seat on the rolling stool. "How are you, sir?"

"Fine. As always. Just getting older."

Dr. Ellers chuckled as he looked at the chart on the computer.

"And yet, I'm happy with what I'm seeing here, so whatever you are doing to stay young, it's working. Keep it up."

"Thanks. I intend to."

"Let's just go over a few things and get you out of here," the doctor said, his eyes reflecting the harsh glow of the screen as he scrolled through the chart. "Labs look good, no new medications, no major complaints to speak of, I see," he said, almost to himself.

Felix noted the thinning gray hair combed unsuccessfully on the doctor's head. With deliberate care, Felix ran his fingers through his own thick waves, grateful for his good hair genes.

"Nope, nothing to complain about," Felix said hopefully, taking a personal bet to see if he could end this appointment in the next two minutes.

"Ah, but your blood pressure needs retaking. Seems that gave Heidi some trouble?"

"Uh, yeah. I suppose so."

"She's the best. That never happens to her." Wheeling himself closer, the doctor fidgeted with the velcro on the cuff. "Anything on your mind? Anything that might have messed that up?" Dr. Ellers probed, his eyes now fixed on Felix.

Felix shrugged. Tried to look casual.

"Nothing leaps to mind."

Except the arch of Sabine's back. The 'v' that appeared at the base of her throat as she threw her head back when she...

That rush of feelings swept over Felix again. Tamped them down.

"No new exercise routines? New vitamins or supplements?"

Felix waved his head in the negative.

"Are you sexually active?"

Dr. Ellers didn't flinch. He wasn't sugar coating it. He asked that question the same way he had asked the others. But it sounded pointed all the same.

"N—" Felix started to say, but then caught himself. "A bit," he amended. He could feel his heart racing in his chest.

Does Sabine really warrant all this attention? What's going on? Probably just the fact that I hadn't gotten any in... how long has it been?

Dr. Ellers smiled, almost conspiratorially.

"Okay then. Good to know. Are you being safe?"

The question stumped Felix for a second. Why would he need to be safe?

The doctor read his confusion. "You'd be surprised these days. People over 55 are the fastest-growing population for STIs. So... just be careful out there."

Felix got the impression that Dr. Ellers fought back an urge to give him a friendly chuck on the shoulder but stopped himself at the last second.

"Will do, Doc," Felix said, hoping against hope that the visit would soon be over.

"Let's run that blood pressure once more, and then we're done. Gotta get you back out there," Dr. Ellers said, a wry smile on his face.

Felix nodded and rolled up his sleeve. This time he would think of England, of Maggie Thatcher, of his second grade math teacher. Anything to get that damn machine to work and get him out of here, once and for all.

Whatever had happened with Sabine was clearly in the past. He was damned if it was going to mess up his future.

He stuck out his arm.

"Fine. Let's get her done."

Chapter 14

Laying Low... but not really

"Pale blue or robin's egg blue?" Sabine murmured to herself, holding up the two books to the afternoon light.

Both volumes looked almost exactly the same—or maybe she was imagining it? Did it matter? Would it really make a difference? What was she doing this project for anyway? Why couldn't she make up her mind?

"Argh!" she cried, hurling both books to the floor. Though she couldn't tell the difference in color between the books, there was one thing she knew for certain: it was a fool's errand to attempt to sort her personal library by color.

But she was running out of ideas to keep herself occupied. She could only be a hermit for so long. Her isolation—self-imposed and comforting as it had been—was starting to wear thin, and she knew she had to get out. If only to get some fresh air and stretch her aching legs. She'd been on her knees most of the day sorting through her immense collection of art books, fiction, poetry, and cookbooks.

So many cookbooks.

Quickly shedding her sweatpants and t-shirt, she threw on a loose but pretty lavender maxi dress that felt silky against her skin. Pairing it with a wide-brimmed hat and huge sunglasses, she smiled to think they offered some measure of anonymity—something that might help with her first venture outside of her house in days.

She'd lost count, really.

It was time. Past time, probably.

The first few minutes after she left the house were glorious. She admonished herself for not getting out sooner. The air was fresh, tinted with salt and citrus, and the sun warmed her exposed shoulders and arms without making her worry about getting a burn. It felt good to stretch her muscles, and the breeze grazing past her neck.

Just a mile and then home. Maybe I'll work on the garden today, she thought, more energy already seeping into her tired heart. Who knew just stepping outside could work such wonders?

The path ahead of her was clear. No walkers, and best of all—no golf carts. She might just be able to avoid people entirely for her brief outing.

"Hellllooooo, gorgeous!"

Like a needle scratching on a vinyl record, Sabine's peace evaporated. The voice—piercing and nasal—came from behind her. She hadn't even seen it coming.

Stopping to turn, Sabine took in the sight of Debbie Carruthers—activities coordinator and Dead-Inside woman of Star Light. She stood in the middle of the path a few feet away from Sabine, her coral pink and aquamarine ensemble garish even for Florida standards.

How could I possibly have missed her?

Waving those neon green nails at Sabine as she hurried over, presumably to latch onto Sabine before she could bolt.

Whatever lack of awareness Debbie might have possessed, she certainly knew how to close in on someone before they could escape.

"Well, aren't you a sight for sore eyes! Haven't seen you around lately. You okay? Have you been sick?"

Debbie's face creased with mock concern—although Sabine knew that sickness at Star Light was as common as the little lizards that lived in every corner of the place.

"No, no, I'm all right. Just been... doing things," Sabine said quickly, wondering if there was any way she could retreat to the safety of her house. Debbie blocked the path. There was no way out but through, and Sabine was not going to run through someone as imposing as Debbie.

"Well, spill it then. What are you up to?" Debbie asked, but before Sabine could answer, Debbie carried on. "Oh! You just have to come with me to the Comm Center with me. There's a lunch happening you just don't want to miss!"

Sabine knew protesting would be futile, and lunch prepared by someone else might not be a bad idea. She was getting tired of cooking just for herself.

With heavy steps, she dutifully followed Debbie, who was more than content to chatter the whole way about the spring calendar at Star Light, the improvements to the crafting center, and the controversy over expanding the visitor's lot.

"Some residents worry that it will mean freeloading grandchildren will be here all summer, taking up space in the pool and having rowdy parties. But others aren't so sure..."

Sabine only half listened, letting Debbie's constant patter wash over her, occasionally throwing in an 'mm-hmm' or a 'that's nice' just to make an attempt at being engaged.

Thankfully, the walk to the Comm Center was short,

and they soon arrived to find a crowd of ladies gathered in the main room. Tables were set up in clumps, and everyone had apparently received a memo to wear soft colors and lots of perfume. The air was practically hazy with it.

Sabine noticed that the room was almost entirely made up of the women of Star Light—the few men she spotted were either staff or a begrudging husband sitting grumpily in a corner.

"I think we're just in time!" Debbie said with glee, her fingers clicking together in a clap. Sabine stood on her toes to see further into the room, and indeed, Debbie seemed to be right. A voice called out, "Get seated, everyone. The presentation is about to begin."

Sabine's stomach dropped. What had been a mild curiosity—and admittedly a ploy for a free lunch she didn't make herself—was in danger of turning into something else. A lecture? On what? Or worse... a timeshare opportunity? Just what had she walked into?

Sabine was happy to see Debbie float away, her attention snagged by women of much higher standing than Sabine could muster. Besides, after days of self-imposed hermitude, Sabine was nervous about being so near the people of Star Light and hoped that sitting in the back would keep her incognito while she grabbed a free lunch.

The gathered ladies, all preening and buzzy, took their seats, and Sabine found a chair in the back. Mercifully no one had spotted her, and those involved in the Streetcar rehearsals were nowhere to be seen.

But the GGs were.

In fact, they were the center of attention. As always. Sabine should have known better than to expect anything else.

With everyone seated, Sabine had a clearer view of the

middle of the room, where a podium had been set up and a table of brochures and papers was displayed. Sabine swallowed. It was a sales pitch. She knew it. Looking at the exit, she wondered if she could sneak away, but it was filled with waiters hustling in with the first course.

Her stomach growled, and she quickly decided she would wait until she had some food and then would quietly sneak out the back.

As expected, Grace and the other GGs flitted about, their hands flying, their earrings glinting. Strangely though, Helen seemed to be the center of attention rather than Grace. Sabine's curiosity won out over her fear of being seen.

What was Helen—the mousiest GG of them all—doing in the limelight?

She even appeared to have had her red dye job touched up for the occasion. It almost looked like a shade a real human would wear.

Sabine chastised herself for being petty and bit down on some endive.

Helen stepped up to the podium, and the room hushed.

"Everyone, thanks for being here. I'm sure you're all excited to meet our guest today. I'm always excited to see him, but then I might be biased," Helen quipped, eliciting polite laughter. "Be prepared to take notes and come with questions—I know you're just going to love what he has to say. Please welcome SunCoast Bank's latest Vice President and my son, Thad Varallo!"

A young man stepped forward. He had been hidden behind a clump of people, but as he stepped up to the podium Sabine could see why the ladies of Star Light were so fizzy.

He was simply gorgeous. Hollywood pretty, with a

mane of dark brown hair, perfect teeth, and purple-blue eyes that glittered even from across the room. His impeccable summer suit hung off a very muscly frame, and he walked with a confidence that only the very beautiful possess.

He leaned over theatrically and gave his mother an exaggerated kiss on the cheek, gaining a hum of approval from the women.

Then, stepping to the microphone, he purred, "Thanks, Mom. You *are* biased, but look where it's got me! Isn't this the most gorgeous assembly of women in the great state of Florida?"

Sabine almost spit out her endive, but shockingly, the compliment worked on more than one woman present, as there was a collective twitter of blushing female senior citizens.

Are we not immune to this crap by now?

Apparently not.

Though, Sabine had to admit his style, confidence, and silky baritone voice were the whole package, and she was curious enough to watch him speak. The content, however? Questionable at best.

"Let's talk about what Sun Coast Bank has done for people in the past and what it can do for you smart women now..."

Sabine listened with the curiosity of someone who appreciates a thing of beauty but not the substance. It was more fascination than allure.

Clearly, she was in the minority. When she really listened to what he had to say—about investment returns and dividends and shareholder opportunities—something in her brain tripped. She wasn't an expert in investing by any stretch, but living with Colin had taught her a thing or two, and she knew that whatever this nepo-baby Adonis was selling, she didn't want it.

Evidently others did.

Twenty minutes went by. During that time, Sabine was able to finish her salad, move on to the salmon and couscous course, complete with a passionfruit tart and cucumber-mint water.

During it all, she witnessed woman after woman stand up, take a brochure off the table, and promptly hand Thad's assistant (a young, forgettable-looking man in a bad suit) hastily scribbled checks. Soon enough, the assistant had an entire portfolio stuffed with them.

Thad was making his mother proud, if not his bank. Helen beamed from her place of importance at a table near the podium, surrounded by the GGs, who nodded at each woman who paid their tithe.

Sabine had to make her exit before they noticed her and added her omission of a personal check to her list of sins.

Pushing her plate away and taking one last sip of water, she stood up to leave, hoping to serpentine her way past the gaggle of waiters waiting to clear the last of the dessert plates.

Her heart plummeted as she felt a tap on her shoulder. Turning, she was faced with a sight she did not expect in the least.

It was Felix, his face creased in irritation, his eyes drilling into the young banker, who was now surrounded by a gaggle of women all eager to be near him.

"Hi, Felix—" Sabine started to say, but he cut her off.

"This isn't working for me. I'm leaving. You can come with me if you want."

The bluntness of this man, the sharp puncture of his words, and his utter disregard for manners left Sabine speechless. Also, she knew he was right. And she wanted to leave too.

She closed her mouth and followed, both of them weaving their way through the staff and out into the Florida sunshine.

So, this is what happens when I leave my house? Maybe I should come out more after all.

Chapter 15

Getting to Know You—for Real This Time

"I'm parked over there," Felix said, pointing vaguely towards a cluster of golf carts on the side of the building.

"Guess we're not walking then, huh?" Sabine asked, testing Felix's mood. She had a feeling that such a question might annoy him or entice him, and honestly, she couldn't begin to guess which way he'd go.

To her relief, he gave her a sly smile and said, "Get in. Maybe I'll surprise you."

Understatement of the year. All this man does is surprise me.

She climbed in next to him, suppressing the cagey feeling that yet again she was fraternizing with the enemy, and pulled the small safety belt on.

Felix looked at her, his eyebrows knitted. "You really think I'm gonna drive so badly you'll need that?"

"Hey! I've seen what you do on this thing. I was almost road pizza once, wasn't I?"

Felix merely clucked his tongue and started up the cart, which was a little anticlimactic given that the electric motor barely made a sound. Nevertheless, soon they were whizzing along the pathway, and the awkwardness of the pitch lunch and all those desperate women fawning over a man decades younger than them all fell away.

Sabine was glad she's jumped at the chance to escape with Felix. Who knows how long it would have taken for the GGs to notice her and pull her into their web?

The two of them rode in silence for a couple of minutes before she felt Felix's shoulders drop a little and his jaw unclench.

"You okay?" she asked, keeping her tone light and casual.

"Yeah," he grumbled. "Just annoyed that Star Light allows these charlatans in here. That guy is no good."

"You think so? I just didn't want to get sucked in. He seemed harmless, though."

Felix merely grunted, and Sabine decided to drop it altogether. It was easy to do as Felix was driving on a path she'd never seen before.

"Where are we headed?" she asked, letting her hand drop from her lap and trail along in the breeze created by the cart.

The sun was starting to slant along the horizon, cutting long shadows through the banyans and palms. Orange and apricot light danced between the shadows, creating lanes of color.

"You'll see," was all Felix said in reply, his eyes locked on the path ahead, both of his hands resting at precise ten and two positions on the small steering wheel. A lock of his silver hair flew back in the breeze, and his pale linen shirt clung close to his chest. Sabine made herself look away—too confused by their dynamic to let herself get distracted.

Isn't this what the kids call vibing? Are we vibing right now?

She honestly couldn't tell.

Instead, she let herself be driven. It had been a lonely few days, and she was glad to be outside, enjoying the late afternoon light, the heat of the day ebbing away.

Minutes ticked by, and Felix drove the cart along a long, winding path that skirted the edge of the entire village. Sabine had never come out this far. Here, the houses were fewer, the raw nature of the original land was far more visible—a snapshot of how things must have looked before hordes of white people clad in pastel and gold jewelry descended on it.

The cart slowed as the path started to incline. The little engine whirred, straining against gravity.

"Come on, girl, come on," Felix muttered under his breath, pushing the cart to keep going.

Sabine worried she might have to get out and push, but just as she was about to say something, the hill crested and they came to a small viewing area. A strip of concrete and gravel that looked out over a large valley.

Below them was a riot of untamed nature—mangrove trees, banyans, and palms, along with various shrubs and bushes—a patchwork of green punctuated here and there with pops of color from the odd flower bloom. It looked wild and a little frightening. Sabine was delighted.

"I didn't know this was here!" she exclaimed.

"No one does. Except the developers," Felix said, a touch of sadness in his voice.

"You mean...?"

"Maybe. I hope not. But they always find places like this at some point. So, for now, all I can do is share it with..."

He trailed off, his eyes trained resolutely forward. Sabine decided not to probe.

"I'm glad you shared it with me. Thank you."

Felix nodded and turned off the cart and got out. "Come on, there's more to see."

Stepping out of the cart, Sabine followed Felix to the edge of the path, where, much to her surprise, a smaller footpath went down the hill and into the dense foliage.

Only the smallest part of her hesitated—could this man be taking her somewhere dangerous?

She squelched the thought and followed him down the path, placing her steps carefully. The fabric of her dress whisked and whispered over the outstretched leaves that hugged the tiny trail.

She needn't have feared, it turns out. Once the hill ended, the terrain was easier than it looked from above, and they wandered at an easy pace—Felix slightly ahead. Sabine drank it all in, the dappled leaves, the sun-kissed colors of the waning day.

As sunset approached, the entire scene took on a saturated air—the colors drenched and full.

"I love this time of day. I wish I could capture it on canvas," Sabine remarked.

"Why don't you?" Felix asked over his shoulder, his hand reaching out to push away a large palm frond blocking their way.

"Oh, I can't," she demurred. "I gave up painting a long time ago."

"Shame," he replied. "I've seen the work you did for the show. You have talent. You should do it more often."

He stopped walking to say this, looking fully into her eyes. His face was calm and open—with just a hint of an invitation written in it.

An invitation to what? Sabine wondered. *Why does this man constantly surprise me?* Everything he did was unpredictable. Did she really even know him at all?

With her cheeks warming, Sabine nodded. "Maybe I will..."

Smiling slightly, Felix nodded and resumed walking. They didn't go much further before the path ended in a small clearing. A mess of rocky outcroppings covered in vines and mosses blocked their way.

"That's it for this trail," Felix explained. "After this part, it gets a little unruly. We should turn back." He moved to do so, but Sabine put out a hand.

"Hang on a second. I'd like a minute to just..." Tipping he head back, she inhaled deeply, sighing out a long, contented breath. "I'm glad you showed it to me. I never would have seen it otherwise. I like knowing that it's here."

They stood, side by side, surrounded by the cul-de-sac of rocks and raw nature. The peace of it washed over her, settling her even in the company of this thoroughly confusing man.

She could hear his breathing—steady and sure. Her nose picked up the musky tang of his scent, a mixture of cologne and that skin she recalled from their night together.

Deep inside her, a small flame ignited. She ignored it. She didn't know where they both were in relation to each other right now, and she didn't want to risk breaking the delicate balance of whatever the next few moments held. So, she stayed still, waiting for Felix to make the next move.

"There are other spots I could show you," he said, taking a small step towards her. "If you'd like?"

His mouth parted slightly, and she could see the redness of his tongue, the sharp glint of his white teeth. The flame in her guts flickered again—more insistently this time.

"I'd like that," she replied, her voice slightly husky.

The moment, like the slightly humid breeze, hung between them for just longer than comfortable before a skittering from the underbrush grabbed her attention. Turning towards it with a small gasp, Sabine saw a small lizard poke its head out. When she turned back to Felix with a breathy laugh, she saw whatever potential the tension between them held had fractured and could not be restored.

Felix cleared his throat. "We should get back. Don't want to be out here when it gets dark."

He was right—the golden-hued afternoon was losing its dominance over the day. Ribbons of lilac and navy had begun to creep in, erasing the path. For a brief moment, Sabine felt a stubborn sort of anger, which she immediately felt foolish over. Why was she angry at the passage of time? Why was she angry that the day was moving into night and ending her time with Felix? She shook her head and whisked the anger away.

The hike back was quicker, Felix setting a brisk pace to keep ahead of the sunset. Sabine was just a little winded when they reached the top, and the cart was a welcome sight.

"Hop on in," Felix said, climbing into the driver's seat.

Soon, they were making their way back along the pathways that Sabine actually recognized, the lights of the houses starting to flicker on.

But the beauty of the walk stayed with her—the knowledge that even Star Light had hidden magic and that Felix Crenshaw was willing to share it with her. It felt like a secret. One that she could nurture and return to when the nights got too long. When loneliness hovered at the edges of her sleep.

"Well, here we are," Felix announced, and Sabine was shocked back into the present, realizing she had daydreamed all the way back.

Stepping out, she hesitated.

Should I invite him in?

Felix remained seated, his body betraying no signs of following.

"Good night, Sabine," he said, a curl of formality in his voice.

She had her answer. He did not wish to be invited in.

She tried not to dwell on it, choosing instead to recall the colors of their walk together.

"Goodnight, Felix. And thank you. I didn't know how much I needed to be out today."

He said nothing in return but merely nodded and gave a small wave.

She opened her front door and waved back, watching him drive into the approaching darkness before locking the door behind her.

What a strange and wonderful afternoon, she thought.

Perhaps I should get out more often.

Chapter 16

A Grand Day Out

"This is NPR," the announcer said, launching into the national news report at the top of the hour. Sabine sighed contentedly, the first buzz of the morning's coffee settling into her bloodstream. Wrapping her fingers around her favorite mug, she looked out at the back garden, speckled in the half light and shadow of the morning.

Knock knock knock.

Sabine's serenity vanished, replaced with confusion. Why would someone knock when there's a doorbell?

Retying her bathrobe and pushing down any stray hairs from her bedhead, she left the kitchen and headed to the front door, opening it only a fraction. She was fairly certain Star Light did not allow solicitation, but perhaps someone had snuck in? Or was Debbie coming for a surprise visit?

It was neither of those things. Peeking out, she got another surprise—one more in a long list.

Felix Crenshaw stood on her doorstep, a look of casual confidence on his face, as if he thought she was expecting him.

"Morning, Felix," Sabine uttered, opening the door

wider and wishing she'd brushed her hair before greeting him. "Didn't expect you here!"

Felix nodded, his eyes matching his pale blue polo shirt, paired perfectly with cream-colored shorts. A large, expensive watch flashed on his wrist.

"We've still got those places to see. The places I promised," he replied, not seeming to register her confusion. "Morning, by the way. You up for it?"

A flutter of excitement and anxiety rushed through her.

Where is he taking me?

Why aren't I dressed?

If I am to go with him, what should I wear?

Why is he even here?

"Can you give me a few minutes?" she stammered in response. "You can come in for some coffee while you wait."

He looked away for a second at his golf cart, the glint of his eye and the set of his jaw unmistakably like James Dean in the famous movie poster.

"Yeah," he mumbled, sighing a little, "sure."

Sabine wasn't sure if he was genuinely annoyed or putting on an act, but she decided not to question it. After all, wasn't he the one who had showed up unannounced and asked her to go outside? Did he think she was just sitting around waiting for something like that to happen?

"Great. Come on in, then," she replied, letting him inside and closing the door. The not-so-distant memory of his last visit to her home loomed large in her mind, but she tried hard to keep her face neutral.

Is he thinking the same thing?

"Milk? Sugar?"

She led him to the kitchen, his sandals making a soft scraping sound as he followed.

"Just black," he said, pulling out a kitchen chair.

"Okay then. Coming right up!" She poured him a cup, silently praising herself for making a larger pot than normal this morning. A happy accident, indeed.

She chose the most boring mug she had, a gray ceramic with a pale blue glaze. It baffled her why such a simple thing would flummox her so much, but whenever Felix was around, she felt a little off-kilter.

She handed over the steaming cup, his gaze lifting to meet hers. For a fraction of a second, their fingertips touched, a small spark transmitting between them.

His hand moved away, placing the mug on the table in front of him.

"Thank you," he said, dropping his eyes.

She cleared her throat.

"So, I'm going to get dressed. But... into what?"

It was an effort to make the question sound casual, like she wasn't making it a proposition—something that could be construed as spicy.

He answered too quickly to have thought that was her intention.

"Something you can walk in. But something that inspires you. Makes you feel comfortable. Also, pack your painting kit."

"My what?"

Felix shrugged as if she should have known what they were talking about.

"You know, your kit. Brushes, paints, whatever. We're going to find you a pretty place to paint."

His eyes fixed on hers, unabashedly searching through her, a look of affection mixed with something else. Compassion, perhaps?

"But... why? Sabine began.

"Because I think your talent shouldn't go to waste."

His attention didn't waver. She held it in return.

Simple enough. And yet it was packed with so much else. He had done it again—managed to surprise her utterly and completely.

She smiled and took one more sip of her coffee.

"All right then. Give me fifteen minutes."

~

They weren't in the golf cart for long. Felix drove Sabine to the other side of the Star Light property. It was yet another place she had not seen or even really knew about. A hidden pocket of dense trees, tangled and knotty, woven together with Spanish moss in a dizzying array of greens and whites.

"Do you feel inspired by that?" Felix asked, pointing at the quiet, almost hushed pocket of nature hidden in all the development.

"I'm... not sure," Sabine replied shyly, her hands playing over the worn handles of the tote bag she had thrown together. It carried a sketchbook, some pastels and pencils, and a nearly depleted watercolor set with a ratty brush. Part of her was embarrassed to show Felix her so-called art supplies.

He'll never think I had any interest or talent at all if he sees this...

If this answer annoyed Felix, Sabine couldn't tell. He merely shrugged and turned back to the golf cart. Sabine followed, relieved but more nervous than ever. At some point, she had to at least pretend she was inspired.

The scene was beautiful, though, and had she been less nervous, she could have easily painted something—an abstract perhaps, of narrow bands of sage, olive, cream, and gunmetal gray. She could practically see the painting materialize before her eyes.

It faded, however, as she returned to the cart and Felix started it up again.

This time, they did not go to another piece of pretty scenery. They wound their way to what Sabine supposed must have been Felix's house—a small, sedate gray-green bungalow, with a well-maintained garden and almost no other decoration whatsoever.

Looks like the kind of place he would live, Sabine thought.

They didn't go inside, but instead Felix invited Sabine, via a gracious opening of the door to his Audi SUV. It was a luxurious ombre blue, with creamy brown leather seats. Sabine felt she was being embraced from behind as she settled into the passenger seat. She allowed herself to sigh loudly as Felix made his way to the driver's side. He didn't need to know how comfortable she was.

Clicking his seatbelt, Felix announced, "Have to go further afield today."

A small pang of anxiety made Sabine's stomach clench momentarily, but he had been such a gentleman so far and her seat was so comfortable, she shooed it away. Besides, her curiosity was piqued. It surprised her to realize how little she had traveled outside of the confines of Star Light since moving in.

Felix drove confidently but not cockily, allowing drivers to merge in front of him and stopping without jerking. Colin, Sabine recalled, had been an impatient, distracted driver, one of the few things she had tried to change about him.

Sabine happily looked out of her window as they left Star Light and entered the surrounding suburbs and more built up areas that collared it. Rows of shopping areas, endless miles of storage facilities, and some patches of downright unpleasant-looking industrial areas. Living at Star Light, it was easy to forget that the world isn't always manicured and maintained.

They headed to a small park, which had a tiny nature preserve nestled into it. It was pretty but much the same as she had previously seen. Her tote bag remained unopened and unexplored.

"Next one, then," Felix said, a note of anticipation in his voice. He seemed pleased she was discerning about what she wanted to capture.

If only he knew it's just because of nerves...

They headed east, towards the shoreline. Felix opened the moonroof, and the salty air flew in, at once comforting and dangerous. The sea had always had that effect on Sabine—something beautiful but also something to be feared.

They stopped at a lookout point perched over the gulf. Below, the waves crashed and hurled themselves at the man-made sea wall, their tips cloudy and sky-blue against the inky blackness of the surrounding water.

It was radiant. Majestic even. But it did not make Sabine open her bag.

Felix fixed her with a determined gaze.

"I've only got one more left," he said. There was an air of challenge in his tone. Sabine's nerves increased. Was this a test? Would she fail? If so, what would that mean? And why did she even care?

Chapter 17

Not So Awkward Adventures

Her perfume had filled the car. It was subtle, but every breath Felix took was filled with her scent. A mix of floral and musk.

He didn't mind. In fact, he found himself taking deeper and deeper breaths as they drove away from Star Light. The smell of her only added to his mission. He was determined to find the perfect spot for her, and he had saved the best for last.

He only hoped she would approve.

What if she doesn't? A small voice nagged at him.

He shook his head imperceptibly as he took a right turn onto a more secluded road that hugged the edge of the ocean.

Not possible, he assured himself. This one had to be the winner.

Sabine stretched a little in her seat. Felix could tell she was enjoying the buttery leather upholstery. Out of the corner of his eye, he stole a glance of her body as it moved.

"This weather is unreal sometimes," Sabine remarked,

her voice languid. "It still surprises me. Even after all these months."

"Yeah, that's Florida for you," he replied, knowing that this reply would lead to precisely nowhere. It wasn't that he didn't want to talk to Sabine. It was that he didn't want to spend precious minutes with her talking about the *weather*.

Sabine seemed to sense this and pivoted. Her gaze remained fixed out the passenger window as he zipped down the road. It was lined with scrubby palm trees and grasslands waving gently in the wake of the car's movement.

"I'm still getting used to the place. The weather, the bugs, those little lizards that dart out at you. It's all so different than what I was used to up north," she said.

"I know. It will get easier with time," he replied.

He had only been in Florida a few months longer than Sabine, but he was very familiar with this feeling of adjustment. He knew that time was the only thing that made living in such a strange climate—hot and humid with a constant threat of deadly storms—the new normal.

Sabine nodded.

"I suppose so. There have been times when I didn't think I could stay here," she said, a slight note of sadness in her voice.

Felix had a sense of why Sabine said this. Could see the tiny door she was opening to him. A chance to explore further.

But he didn't want to take it. It was too unwieldy. It might ruin the delicate balance of the goal before him. He wanted her to focus only on this trip, on being in the right headspace for painting.

I have to prove why she should stay, and my words won't do it. Only actions will, an emphatic voice said in his mind.

He bit his lip in confirmation. Another second went by, and he realized she was waiting for a response.

"It will get better. I promise."

He said the words with conviction. Hoping it would set her at ease.

She leaned back in her seat and looked at him. Her gaze was steadfast and warm, and Felix was well aware of it. Though the road was getting increasingly wild and bumpy, he slowed down a bit and turned slightly to her.

"I believe you. I just need time. And... friends to make it easier," she concluded.

He gave her a smile and a nod. Turned his eyes back to the road.

"I think that can be arranged," he replied.

And he meant it. He wanted her to be happy. To feel secure. For her to want to stay in this place.

But why? For himself? For her? Because it seemed like a natural next step in someone's life?

No, it's more than that. And you know it, the voice murmured.

Felix didn't panic at the thought. Didn't feel anxiety or protest.

If anything, it all felt right. Natural, even.

"I'll hold you to it, then," Sabine said, smiling in his peripheral vision.

She was facing front once more, taking in the view that was quickly unfolding as they neared their destination.

"You're on," he replied.

Silence dropped between them, but it wasn't awkward or odd. It was just... present.

Felix kept driving. They would soon be there.

And he just hoped she'd be impressed.

Chapter 18

Plein Air

The drive took longer than she expected—perhaps forty minutes. The car hummed along, seemingly happy for the outing. People didn't drive in actual cars all that much while at Star Light.

They chatted, and, as usual, Felix replied with the bare minimum. Yet, Sabine never felt the need to pry or dig deeper. Nor did she feel it from Felix. If anything, a sense of ease nestled between them. The kind that didn't require words. They could sit in companionable silence as the car took them to... wherever Felix was headed.

Finally, Felix turned from the main road and onto a narrow, one-lane track that needed repair. The SUV bumped and skipped along before coming to a stop at a dead end. Sea grasses and small shrubs bent in unison against a strong breeze blowing west off the water. The gulf itself lay before them like a shining ribbon just under the horizon.

"No one ever comes here," Felix said, pride in his voice as he cut off the ignition.

"Remember where we parked," he said, smirking.

Sabine giggled, happy to see him so happy. He was not a man who showed that emotion easily, it seemed, and something about this place brought it out of him.

He moved quickly to open her door, and she stepped out, the tote bag in her left hand. Her mirth lessened slightly as the pressure to feel inspired returned. Sabine had always been a people pleaser and Felix had gone to all this trouble...

But I didn't ask him to do this.

She stepped out, relishing the crunch of fine white sand under her sandals. Her long skirt whipped against her legs, along with long tendrils of sea grass.

"Careful, the wind is pretty strong, but it's not cold," Felix said.

"Got it," she replied.

Felix led her to a dirt path that was barely visible in the grass. It sloped downwards, the scrub holding the sand at bay. Still, it was precarious, and the wind was persistent. Felix held out his hand to help Sabine make her way down.

After a few feet, the slope evened out, and Sabine found herself on a tiny strip of beach. As if someone had flicked a switch, the wind stopped, or rather, it was prevented from getting to her by the slope of the hill. The world became instantly quieter, the only sound being the lull of the waves and the call of distant seabirds.

"How...?" Sabine marveled.

"Amazing, isn't it?" Felix said. "It's almost like a magic trick."

He was right. This tiny spit of land was totally hidden and utterly sheltered. The sea was azure blue, the waves as gentle and sedate as if they'd been told to behave. Even if only for this moment and this place.

A fallen log, polished from rolling in the sea, lay on the

sand, and Felix invited Sabine to sit with him there. She did so, basking in the warmth of the sun on the wood. She closed her eyes for some moments, savoring the warmth, the fresh air, and the magic of this place.

When she opened them, she saw Felix looking at her, a kind of expectation written on his face.

"Well?" he asked. "How about this one?"

Her nerves flared once more, but it was not a hard decision. This scene she had to capture. And if the effort was poor, so be it. She had to try. For herself as well as to reward Felix for the gift of bringing her here.

"Yes, I think this will do," she said, laughing.

Felix slapped his hands on his thighs in approval.

"Good! Glad to hear it."

They sat, looking at each other, both feeling the myriad potential of the next few seconds. Would she create the beginnings of a masterpiece? Or something she would hide in regret and shame? Or would he say something meaningful, something apart from the small talk of the day? Or... would something else happen?

It hovered, unanswered, for a moment longer, and then Sabine pulled open her bag.

"There you go," Felix breathed, a bit of satisfaction in his voice.

"I'm not sure what I'm doing!" Sabine laughed, pulling out the sketchpad and her meager supplies. If Felix judged them, he was kind enough not to give it away.

"You know more than you think," was all he said in reply, turning away from her to look at the view.

"Hardly," Sabine said, though she gave it her best effort, which was tricky, given the terrain. She set up a small container of water (basically a reused yogurt cup) on the flattest part of the log she could find and then the paints next to it.

She was going for abstract, she knew that much. Might be a bit easier to justify any heinous errors.

Finally, when all was set up, she lifted her eyes, trying to figure out her first move. It was intimidating to look at the white expanse of creamy paper perched on her knee, its emptiness demanding attention. But what? What would be the first brushstroke? It could make or break whatever she did next.

So, she looked. The sky merged with the sea at some unknowable distance, a blurry, hazy mashup of blues and whites. The foreground was nothing but sea, occasionally dotted by wispy cirrus. And lastly, the tiny nib of the land at her feet, drawing a chalky brown line along the whole perspective.

With a slightly trembling hand, she lifted her brush and dipped it in the water. A wash was needed, just a hint of cobalt tint in it to set the scene.

She mixed the color, lifted it towards her sketchbook, and looked once more at the scene before her. Then, Felix jumped forward, a goofy expression on his face. Sabine shrieked and laughed in surprise.

"Ah! Are you photobombing my landscape?"

Felix laughed in return.

"Yup! Guess I am!"

Once again, he had shocked her. He didn't seem the type to do such a thing, but then again, nothing he had done had any sort of pattern or plan, at least according to her.

This was a delightful discovery.

"I'm not sure I can do you justice!" Sabine retorted, her brush dripping color onto the log.

"I'll get out of your way, I promise!"

He moved away, walking a few lazy steps to admire the view.

She returned to her painting, her nerves thoroughly gone. Was that why he had done it? Made her laugh to dispel her anxieties?

Whatever that was about, it had worked, and she happily splashed color on the page, nursing it, teasing it, coaxing it into something resembling a painting.

"May I see?" Felix said, shocking Sabine out of her concentration.

To her utter amazement, she discovered almost an hour had passed. It had felt like mere minutes. The light was beginning to change, and she could see what she had captured was already memory only.

"Um... yes, I think so," Sabine replied, hesitantly turning the sketchpad towards him.

He said nothing for a long while, his eyes looking intently.

"It's... wonderful. Truly. You do have talent." His gaze lifted to hers, swirling with heat and approval. The hint of a naughty smile in the corner of his mouth. "I knew it."

A warm flush glowed in Sabine's cheeks. She didn't know she had wanted a compliment so badly until it was given, simply and genuinely, from this complete enigma of a man. Possibly a man who had a dark past, something she didn't know anything about but could only guess.

It was all so confusing, and yet, that compliment filled her.

"I... thank you," deciding at the last minute to not demure, to not apologize it away, but simply to accept his praise.

"Did you enjoy making it?"

He stood close to her, the wind shifting his shirt around on his body, his hands clasped behind his back.

"I did. Time didn't really mean anything for a while."

Felix smiled and nodded.

"Something we're always seeking, isn't it? Glad you found it. At least, for a little bit."

She looked at him, a shadow obscuring his face, and then away to the ever-changing sea.

"Mmm, yes, I suppose. Thank you."

She packed up her supplies, and they made their way back to the Audi, its interior hot from baking in the sun.

Within a few moments, the car's glorious A/C cooled them down as Felix expertly backed down the track and onto the main road once more.

The drive back to Star Light was quiet but not awkward. After the A/C had done its work, Felix let the windows down so the breeze came in. Sabine was content to let her hand trail out the window, her hair flying.

As with all journeys, the return seemed to take less time than setting forth, and soon she found herself back in her own little driveway.

The afternoon was well advanced, and everything was soaked in the day's sun; the garden's colors popped, and the grass was a more saturated hue. Or maybe it just looked more colorful and entrancing because of her little trip with Felix. She couldn't tell.

Felix opened her car door one last time and held out his hand.

"Thank you," Sabine said, allowing herself to be delivered to her own doorstep.

They stood facing each other, another prickle of possibility hovering over them.

"And thanks for a wonderful day out. I really enjoyed it," she continued.

"You are welcome. Thanks for being adventurous," he replied.

Their eyes met and held. But only briefly.

"Have a great rest of your day, then," he said, stepping away. "I will leave you in peace."

"Oh, you don't have to think that—" she began, but he was already walking back to his car.

"See you soon," he said, opening his car door.

Within a minute, he was gone, his car turning right and heading back to his own home.

Clumsily, Sabine let herself into her house and stood in the foyer, her tote bag swinging from her arm.

"What was that?" she said out loud.

Nothing about him made sense. Nothing about his motives, his surprises, or his aloofness made a lick of sense.

But one thing did.

How dearly she had wanted him to kiss her on the doorstep.

Chapter 19

An Uneasy Alliance

"Sabine! Sabine! Come sit with us!" Topaz called, waving frantically, as if she were guiding a Boeing 747 into its gate.

Though Sabine did her best to pretend she had not heard, it was in vain. She might have been able to dodge one GG (Topaz), but Helen quickly crossed the room—who knew she could move that fast?—and practically accosted her.

I knew I should have stayed at home, Sabine admonished herself.

It hadn't been her intention to go to the Comm Center, but she hadn't bought groceries in a few days, and her stocks were low. A quick lunch before shopping was her only goal. Her Nan had always told her to never go grocery shopping on an empty stomach, and she lived by this rule. Hungry shoppers bought silly things.

Alas, hungry shoppers who stopped by the Comm Center for a quick bite also paid a price.

"Oh! I'm not staying long..." Sabine began to protest, but it fell on deaf ears. Within moments, she was sucked into the vortex that was the GGs' usual spot—i.e., the middle of the Comm Center.

"We haven't seen you in ages," Rebecca scolded, with nods from the others. Grace Pickney sat, as usual, in the center of the hubbub, her eyes boring into Sabine.

"Where have you been lately? And you better dish," she demanded, her words icy under a razor-thin veneer of gentility.

Sabine knew it was useless to pretend she didn't know what they were talking about, but she wasn't about to give Grace—as she had demanded—*the dish*.

"Well, I... I've been busy with lots of things," Sabine began, only to have Grace wave a hand impatiently.

"No, don't play coy. We've all seen you. Or, should I say, seen the both of you? You and that Felix Crenshaw. We've never seen him so active. When he first came here, he was so reclusive, we thought he was a vampire! But you've got him running hither and yon!"

Grace ended her little speech by crossing her arms petulantly. She was clearly miffed that Felix wasn't showing her the same attentions, and she was dying to know Sabine's secret. Or rather, how anyone like Sabine had managed to get so much of Felix' time in the first place.

Sabine sighed inwardly, knowing this was bound to happen. After their day trip to find the perfect painting spot, she and Felix had been spending a bit of time together. What struck her was that it had taken her so long to realize how much other people had noticed.

It wasn't like their excursions were anything fancy or extravagant. Coffee dates at a local café outside of Star Light—trips to the library and one jaunt to the movies. Anything, so long as it was away from the busy Comm Center.

Plus, long walks. Around Star Light, and even along some of the local beaches.

Through it all, Felix had remained aloof. The picture of a perfect gentleman, not touching Sabine or making her feel as though something else was on his mind.

Sabine, for her part, had been glad to get out of the house and visit places that made her happy— reading books and walking had always been some of her favorite things to do. And while Felix wasn't one for much conversation, she enjoyed being with him and the sense of ease that existed between them. True, she didn't know much about his past, but that ease was undeniable.

The nagging questions as to who he had been— especially in relation to Colin—and whether their one-night stand was going to remain exactly that, she pushed to the side.

Most of the time.

Still, there were pockets of their time together that hinted at something more. Where her body gravitated towards his, where she hoped he would lean in just a little closer. Perhaps even look deeply into her eyes once more...

"Just hanging out. Felix and I share a lot of the same interests," Sabine said, adopting her own version of Grace's nonchalant waving motion. "I don't like to drive much, and he does, so that's been helpful."

Sabine held Grace's gaze, daring her to contradict this statement. Grace pursed her lips, assessing Sabine's words.

"*Right,*" she said finally, elongating the word incredulously while looking to the other GGs, who leaned in expectantly.

"Yup! That's all," Sabine said with a shrug of her shoulders. She wasn't going to give Grace anything further.

The sharp-featured woman must have sensed it because in the next moment, she changed the subject.

"You're here for lunch? Alone?" Grace asked.

"Yes, I need to do some grocery shopping soon," Sabine replied, making a move towards the buffet tables.

Topaz responded, "Maybe Felix can drive you to the store."

Like a school of sharks, Topaz thought she had drawn a little blood on Sabine to stir up the waters. Sabine could practically feel the GGs spark with excitement.

"Oh, no. That's just me time. I actually like getting groceries alone." Sabine said, reveling in the obvious deflation from the group.

"Well, do it soon because we have rehearsal tonight, and I heard you are back in the fold," Grace said, refusing to allow Sabine to enjoy her small victory for long.

"Oh... yes, right."

A grim heaviness settled into Sabine's stomach. Even now, she wasn't sure why she had agreed to return to help out on Streetcar, but Jerrold—no doubt coached by Elise— had called Sabine only days before with an apology and a breathy appeal.

They needed help backstage desperately, and while he was sorry that Sabine had been treated 'in an unprofessional manner,' surely they could mend fences and try again?

Sabine could practically feel Jerrold gritting his teeth as he asked Sabine to come back, but they must have been stretched thin. Besides, Felix was also going to help out, and they had agreed to watch out for each other. Without Felix volunteering also, Sabine might never have said yes.

Grace's reminder, however, was ill-timed and put Sabine in danger of losing her appetite.

"See you soon!" Grace said, waving her fingers and

turning back to the girls, already involved in another conversation.

Half-heartedly waving back, Sabine trudged to the buffet area and made herself a plate.

Selecting a table nearest the window, she ate alone, the food not nearly tasting as good as she'd hoped.

Still, she nursed a small flame of excitement.

Tonight, she would be at the theatre, and Felix was going to be there too.

There are worse ways to spend an evening, right?

Chapter 20

Opening Night

"Think they'll get the lines right?" Felix whispered, his hands creating a small opening in the dusty black curtains.

"Maybe. Though not necessarily in the right order," Sabine retorted, pressing her eye to the small gap in the curtain.

From her slivered vantage, Sabine saw the house of the theatre beginning to fill. People waved and called to each other, wafting thin programs in the air and greeting their friends.

As much as she didn't want to admit it, she was excited about opening night. Rehearsals—especially tech—had been long and tiresome, but she was proud of the work she had done on the props and the set.

She was also fortunate that she hadn't been asked to understudy again. Trudy's digestive system had since behaved, and though it went unsaid, everyone seemed pleased about it.

Felix had been with her for most of the rehearsals, helping with carpentry and stringing lighting cable.

Throughout it all, they relied on each other for comic relief.

Whenever Brock flubbed a line in a most spectacular way, Sabine couldn't resist catching Felix's eye for a shared look of utter disdain. Or, when Trudy screeched in what she thought was a dramatic show of emotion, Felix would plug his ears, making Sabine giggle and hide her face.

All in all, she'd started to look forward to her nights at the theatre, rather than dread them as she had before.

Mainly because she knew she would see Felix and the hours would fly by.

"Can't believe they are all here," Felix replied, his voice husky in the dark. "To watch some truly awful acting."

"Aww, come on, Grace isn't that bad," Sabine purred, though they both knew Grace's Blanche was, at best, cringeworthy. Her idea of the faded Southern belle had been built into nothing more than a fawning caricature.

Felix fixed Sabine with an eye cast in shadow and set his jaw.

"Come on, Sabs, you don't have to lie to me now. That's what the actors are for."

Sabine giggled and looked down at her shoes.

When did he start calling me Sabs? And why do I like it?

"Places, everyone, places," Elise called as she whizzed by, knocking on dressing room doors.

Fresh flowers and a bottle of champagne rested on the beat-up table in the backstage area, and a few stagehands— well-meaning men who had no golf game to get to—sat around in folding chairs, waiting for their first cues to raise the curtain or move a prop.

"Guess this is it," Sabine said, pulling her face away from the curtain.

A flicker of excitement shivered through her. The

murmur of the expectant crowd, all the hours that everyone had put in—even the dreadfulness of the actor's performances couldn't stop the feeling of nervous anticipation in the air.

"Guess so," Felix replied. "I gotta get to my station on stage left."

"And I'll hold down stage right," she said.

"Maybe we can make faces at each other across the way," Felix invited, giving her a wink.

"Maybe, but I'm not sure we'll get away with it."

"Can't hurt to try," he said, giving her hand a tiny squeeze before leaving.

Her hand went tingly from his touch, sending a wave of light shooting upwards into her chest.

Has he truly not touched me since that night?

That wasn't entirely true. There were a few moments when he helped her from his car, or their skin grazed as he walked past... but this time the touch was deliberate. He had *chosen* to touch her, chosen to close the gap between them.

Her mind went temporarily blank.

"You're in my spot," hissed Trudy, assuming her position backstage.

Sabine could only nod meekly and retreat to a small area behind the curtain on stage right, armed with the prompt book and a flashlight. She hoped she wouldn't have to use the book. She wasn't sure her head was working right.

As soon as she was in place, the lights dimmed and a hush fell over the crowd. The show was about to begin.

Chapter 21

In the Wings

Sabs? Where did that come from? Felix wondered, taking his place behind the dusty curtain on stage left.

Both his mind and his hand buzzed a little. For different reasons.

His mind reeled at the familiarity he had shown towards Sabine—the cute nickname, the banter, the winks. Who was he in those moments? Was he playing a game? Or, was he truly at ease and everything that had happened was off the cuff and in the present?

Was any of that so bad?

His fingers tingled from the feel of Sabine. It was like his skin seemed to come alive whenever they touched.

When was the last time we touched?

He couldn't believe it had been so long. After all, he thought about touching her so often, it seemed criminal he hadn't actually done it more often.

Wriggling his fingers, he tried to concentrate. One of the board members—a tedious man in a shockingly bad suit —was doing the curtain speech. Soon, Star Light would fall away and the show would begin.

Felix didn't have much to do during the first act. He received a hand off of a prop early on but mostly just stood off stage waiting for the scene change at intermission.

That left nothing but time for his brain to think. Think about Sabine. Think about her growing presence in his life. In his mind. And, perhaps... his heart?

After a jubilant round of applause from the opening night crowd, the lights began to dim and a hush rippled through the theatre. Felix watched dust motes swirl in the dying light before disappearing into a brief darkness.

A moment later, the lights burst back into life, and the play officially began. The actors entered, lines were said, and bodies moved in space.

Felix didn't bother watching. He knew he had time before he had to be useful. Across the stage he gazed into the shadows of the other wing. Just beyond the curtain, he could make out the dim outline of Sabine's oval face, her hair shining slightly in the reflection of the stage lights. She watched the play intently, her mouth moving slightly along with the words. Though they had laughed and teased their way through the rehearsal process and told each other that they thought the whole thing was a big joke, he knew how much she had poured into the process. Could see the effect the whole thing had on her. It made her shine even more brightly.

Her skin shimmered. Or, at least, he thought it did. Her eyes sparkled despite the shadows, and he willed her to look at him. For several long moments, her attention was completely caught up in the action onstage. Her eyes followed the actors, her hands flicking slightly at her sides.

Just look this way, he said silently. *Just one look.*

Then—in a flash—she did. Their eyes connected across the stage, a tiny filament cutting through the world of

Blanche, Stanley, and Stella. For Felix, that world stopped spinning. There was only Sabine, returning his gaze.

"Happy opening," Felix mouthed silently at her, over-enunciating his lips to make sure she got the message.

She shook her head in confusion, her brow furrowing.

"Haaaaa-peeeeee ohhhhhh-pennn-ing," he mouthed again, slower this time.

Her confusion stayed, etching into her pretty features. *When did I start thinking of her this way?*

She waved her hands, as if to erase the broken signal he had sent across. She raised both her hands in a wave and then, seemingly on a whim, blew him an exaggerated kiss.

A bloom of heat rose throughout his chest.

Could that silly girl gesture really have such an effect?

Apparently, she could.

Before he could stop himself, he pretended to catch the kiss and pretended to stagger under its spell.

Sabine made a gulping laugh sound and quickly clapped both her hands over her mouth. Felix clocked a flicker of irritation cross Brock's face, but he quickly turned his attention back to Sabine.

She was still laughing but silently this time, her body vibrating as she fought to control herself.

Felix smiled, letting the bloom grow throughout his body, warming every part of him.

Happy opening, indeed...

Chapter 22

Opening Night Rolls On

"**A**nd of course, none of this would be possible without the countless people backstage and front of house, who make everything run so smoothly. Let's give a hand!"

Jerrold led the applause, and his face was the picture of true gratitude.

It's almost like he's convinced himself, Sabine mused, gripping her plastic flute of cheap champagne.

She could feel the drink's bubbles in her tummy. More importantly, she could feel its effects in her head—that fizzy, giddy feeling of just being on the right side of drunk.

"To the volunteers!" the crowd intoned, raising their glasses.

Wasn't everyone a volunteer?

But Sabine couldn't stay sarcastic for long. Truth was, the opening had gone well. Despite Brock's flubbing of lines. In spite of Trudy's horrendous wailing and, most miraculous of all, Grace's wooden performance couldn't put a damper on the night.

Everyone was in a good mood. The show was open. Only three more performances to go.

They had done it.

Somewhere in the crowd, she knew Felix was making the rounds, gliding easily among the well-wishers and hangers-on. She had somehow lost him in the post-curtain-call chaos backstage.

Perhaps that's for the best, thought Sabine. Her feet were beginning to throb after so much time standing backstage, and she knew if she drank another glass of this truly hideous champagne, she would pay dearly in the morning.

Besides, no one was wishing her a happy opening anyway. She had done her bit, and now it was time to go home. Her purse was in the backstage area. Sighing, she told her tired feet to get moving so she could retrieve it and head home.

Sliding through the crowd, tossing out an occasional hello or good night, she soon made her way to the door that led backstage. Walking through it, the din of the party immediately stilled, a mere hum behind a metal door.

For a brief moment, she closed her eyes and took a deep breath. She loved the smell of wood and paint. Comforting, like her grandfather's workshop when she was a girl.

The whole area was dark, only lit by a few clip lamps with blue gels snapped over their harsh glares. She loved backstage light too. So cozy. Mysterious. Only needed for the most essential of business—quick changes, actors waiting, props being shuffled about.

Taking a moment to let her eyes adjust to the dim light, she closed them for just a second. There was something magical about being backstage, the illusion of the world beyond the curtain, and the reality of its workings behind the facade. It never failed to entrance her—even with such poor actors doing the work.

"Hi there," came a voice.

Sabine shrieked and clutched at her throat, startled nearly out of her skin.

"Oh! You scared me half to death!"

Emerging out of the darkness was Felix, an almost empty champagne flute in his hands.

"Sorry!" he said, holding one hand out in a placating gesture. "I didn't mean to startle you. I just needed a break from all that noise and I just... I love it back here."

"Yet another surprise." As soon as she said it, Sabine clapped a hand over her mouth. She hadn't meant to say that last thought out loud.

"What was that?" Felix leaned in, a sly smile curling the corners of his mouth. She knew she'd been caught.

"I... uh..." she began to lie, but then something clicked within her—a firm resolve.

Why do I keep hiding? Why do I keep censoring my words around this man? What's the harm in speaking the truth?

She knew it might be the bubbles talking, but her boldness couldn't be stopped now that it was being given free reign.

"I... you just continue to surprise me, that's all," she said finally, looking him square in the eye.

"Surprise you? How?"

He seemed genuinely curious—even a little tentative, as if he was anxious about the answer.

"I don't know. I just think you're one way—"

"But I turn out to be another," he said, with an air of familiarity in his voice.

Sabine laughed.

"I guess that's been said to you before."

Felix nodded. "Many times. It might explain my enduring bachelorhood."

He said the words flippantly, but Sabine felt a distinct ring of sadness to it.

"Ah, I see," she said.

"Have I scared you off?" he asked.

She wanted to ask, *from what?* They had barely touched since that night on her couch, but saying it out loud would surely shut down the conversation. Right now, she wanted nothing more than to encourage it.

"Not at all," she replied and, to her surprise, found herself very close to him. In the dim light, their bodies had moved towards each other, like slow-drawing magnets.

"Oh, good," he breathed, his voice slightly growling. A thrill spread from her stomach down to her lower half. His cologne, his body heat, and his sweetly-scented breath mixed with champagne filled her senses, and she closed her eyes briefly to savor it.

"You've always seemed the brave type," he added, his fingers brushing hers as they faced each other. She could feel the biting edge of the prop table behind her as his body pressed forward into hers.

"I am," she said, the only words she could manage before his mouth was on hers, hungry.

Unleashed.

So many weeks of not touching. So many weeks of lost moments, potential moments, moments of possibility that were never realized.

It all added up to this—a huge yearning, finally unbridled and unfettered, washing over them both.

Mouths tugging, overlapping, devouring. Their hands mirrored this eagerness—pulling at clothes, tearing at zippers, fastenings, and shirt tails.

Sabine could hardly breathe—not that she cared. She was nothing but one raw nerve, filling a huge void that had been so empty before. This rising passion, this insatiable need for Felix's skin, his body, his scent, his... *essence.*

With a crash, Felix lifted her up onto the table, sending some props skittering. She made the barest of mental notes to fix them later. After all, wasn't she the expert on them? She had built them and was largely left in charge of their care. She could break them if she wanted to.

Right now, theatre etiquette could go to hell—all she wanted was Felix's hands on her skin, her breasts, her ass...

"Mmm, I missed you," he murmured between kisses, his palms sliding up her back and towards her breasts, deftly slipping beneath her bra.

"So did I..." she replied, her fingers entangled in his hair, pulling him closer to her—as if that were even possible. His mouth drew away from hers, and he bent low to kiss her neck, pushing aside the fabric of her little black dress to expose a breast.

"Mmmm," she groaned as his warm mouth found her nipple.

Am I really doing this? Backstage? In public, almost? Like a teenager?

It only added to the intensity.

Her hands found his zipper, madly scrambling to pull it open, even as he fumbled with the buttons of her dress.

They were mad for each other, almost like love drunk kids. Felix's hands shook every bit as much as hers did, and Sabine trembled to think he wanted her as badly as she wanted him. That they were both so wound up that they didn't care about being clumsy or graceless. That they only wanted each other, an unstoppable force taking over him as much as it had her.

She was wet with pleasure, longing for him. For him to enter her, pushing himself into her over and over again. It was all so close, and she promised herself she would let him have her completely, even here among the dust and the gloom.

"I think I left it in my dressing room..." came a nasal, whining sound from somewhere in the darkness.

Trudy.

With a snap, Felix and Sabine reversed course. As quickly as they had ripped at each other, they began to madly reassemble themselves—pulling buttons, zippers, and sleeves into place. Patting down hair and wiping away their kisses.

"Oh! What are you two doing here?" Trudy asked, stepping into view just as Sabine put a respectable distance between her and Felix. She could only hope her labored, panting breaths weren't obvious.

"Just getting my purse..." Sabine said, her voice an octave too high.

Trudy looked them over, her small, glinty eyes assessing them like a high school principal. Sabine felt herself shrink under the scrutiny.

After what seemed an age, Trudy spoke.

"Uh-huh," came her verdict. She started towards her dressing room. "There's a bunch of props on the floor. You might want to take care of those," she said snootily, resuming her role as the mediocre diva of Star Light theatricals.

"On it," Felix said, giving her a mock salute.

As soon as she disappeared, Sabine clasped her hand over her mouth.

She didn't know if she wanted to laugh or kiss Felix.

She had a suspicion it was a bit of both.

Chapter 23

Shattered

For a few moments, Sabine and Felix merely looked at each other, listening to Trudy's footsteps as she disappeared into her dressing room. A well of laughter sprung up inside Sabine, the type of giddiness she'd felt playing silly pranks back in her school days.

Why does being with Felix always make me feel this way?

Felix held up a finger for them both to keep quiet until they were sure Trudy was out of earshot.

Tears streamed down Sabine's face from the effort of keeping her laughter inside while she took stock. She wanted to kiss Felix and keep kissing him—and do all the other things too—but she also wanted to fall into a heap of braying laughter until waves of delirious joy washed over them both.

What is going on?

She hadn't felt this type of dizzy elation, this feeling of *abandon*, in so long. It seemed wrong somehow. And yet, completely right.

After a few moments of strained silence, Felix let his

finger come down, and Sabine lowered her hand from her mouth and allowed herself to take a deep, shuddering breath.

"Do you think she—" Sabine began to ask.

Felix nodded.

"I'm sure she thinks something. We may be better actors than her and Brock, but we ain't that good."

Sabine giggled, reaching out to twine Felix's fingers with hers. That hunger rose up again, swallowing the laughter. Replacing her fizzy energy with something else. Something primal and demanding.

Clearly, Felix could feel it too. His body moved towards hers, his breath thickened. He leaned in to kiss her...

"Oh no! No, no, no!"

A shrill cry from down the hall snapped Sabine and Felix away from each other yet again.

They looked hastily around, trying to find the source.

"Oh nooooo," came a moan. This time, Sabine was able to clock it: it was coming from Trudy in her dressing room.

Giving Felix a look of confused apology, she headed down towards the sound. Aroused as she was, Sabine couldn't ignore whatever was going on so close by.

She opened her mouth to speak, her hand poised to knock on the dressing room door. She needn't have bothered.

The door opened in a rush, and Trudy appeared, her eyes wild. She clutched her cell phone in her hand.

"I can't believe it! I just can't!" Trudy wailed, looking at Sabine with desperation and panic.

"What's going on?" Sabine asked, but Trudy didn't answer. She brushed past her, heading back out towards the party in the lobby.

As she rushed away, Trudy cried, "Check your accounts. Check all of them!"

By the time she had disappeared, Felix was standing behind Sabine, a look of concern on his face.

"What was that about?" he asked.

"Not sure. Maybe we should go find out."

They shared a look of momentary sadness over the interrupted passion sparking between them, then moved down the hall after Trudy.

When Sabine left the party to retrieve her purse, everything had been in full swing. Conversations bubbled, happy cheers, and the clink of champagne flutes rung out. A raucous shindig by anybody's standards.

Now, however, when they opened the door to rejoin it, the mood had completely soured. People huddled in groups, bent over their phones.

Some were crying. Others gasped. Still others asked the same question repeatedly, "How? How could this happen? This can't be right, can it?"

In the middle of all of this stood the GGs, their faces knitted in collective concern and anguish. Grace, in particular, looked as lost and vulnerable as Sabine had ever seen her. Or could even imagine her looking—and that was saying something.

Walking towards them, she laid a hand gently on Grace's arm.

Grace let out a squeak and turned to face her.

"Oh! You startled me!"

Sabine began to apologize, but Grace cut her off.

"Oh, it's just too much. I can't believe it. Did it happen to you too?"

Grace grasped at Sabine's hands, crushing her fingers slightly.

"Grace, did *what* happen? I'm lost here."

"Your bank account. Is it okay? Check it! Check it right now!"

Grace was almost feral—wild with anxiety and worry. Her sharp fingernails clutched at the sides of Sabine's hands.

Panic lapped at Sabine's stomach.

What is she talking about? Has everyone been scammed or something? Is this all some horrible joke?

Pulling her hands free from Grace's, Sabine took out her phone. Never very good with technology, she fumbled with logging into her account. After a few frustrating tries, she managed to access her primary checking. The one that serviced most of her needs and bills.

Panic quickly melted into a flood of relief as she saw it was largely untouched—her insurance payment had gone through, but that had been expected. Otherwise, it was fine. Healthy as always.

Grace looked at her expectantly.

"Well?" she pleaded.

"I'm fine, Grace. Nothing's happened there."

A sigh escaped Grace—a mixture of relief and jealousy. Sabine took her hand once again.

"Grace—are you telling me...?"

"Our bank accounts are drained. All of us. Nothing left! Oh, what are we going to do? We're senior citizens! How can people do such things? There's a special place in hell..."

She dissolved into tears, and Sabine pulled her close, ignoring the strange irony of comforting this woman who had never seemed to need or want comfort at any time before.

As she did so, she looked around.

The party had become a wake. People left, distraught

expressions on their ashen faces, clutching phones or each other as they vowed action—phone calls to be made. Police to be called.

What she didn't see, however, was Felix.

Where had he gone? Was he affected too?

She didn't have time to wonder. Grace clutched at her, deepening her hug.

Sabine needed to stay where she was needed.

Finding Felix would just have to wait.

Chapter 24

Tensions High

"I'm glad I could help you today. Will that be all?" the friendly woman's voice chirruped in Sabine's ear.

Sabine sighed, grateful yet again that her account had been spared.

And also grateful she had received a different customer service representative. She had, after all, called her bank almost a dozen times in the past forty-eight hours just to be sure her account was safe.

"No, that's all. Thank you. I really appreciate it. I know I can check these things alone, but..."

The woman replied. "Not a problem. Happy to help."

The call ended, and Sabine dutifully took the post-call survey just to thank the kind woman for her time. And infinite patience.

She put her phone down and sat back in her kitchen chair. The accounts were safe. Well, hers, anyway. Nothing had come close to harming them.

That wasn't the case with most of the women of Star Light. There was a chance that some men had been affected, but the only ones she truly knew about were women.

The GGs were no exception. Most of them had seen their accounts emptied out. Only Helen, like Sabine, had been spared.

For two days, there had been no other topic of conversation except the scam that had likely taken a lot of them in. Emails and flyers had been distributed by the staff of Star Light offering financial counseling—no doubt, the management of Star Light was worried about rent payments bouncing and wanted to seem as helpful as possible.

But Sabine didn't have to worry about any of that. Which left her relieved and guilty all at once.

"Maybe I should go out," she said aloud to her empty living room.

Since the show's opening, she had kept a low profile, only venturing out for essentials and to comfort people as she could—which wasn't much. Everyone stayed holed up in their homes, phones glued to their ears, no doubt pleading for the return of their money.

Sabine could have felt superior—smug even—for being spared. But she didn't. And she headed to the Comm Center, hoping she could be useful with a kind word or a shoulder to cry on. Despite the rocky couple of months she'd spent at Star Light, a strange sort of affection had come over her. The notion that perhaps she did have a place in this odd community after all.

Admittedly, knowing Felix was a big part of that as well. *Except I haven't seen him in days. Where is he?*

Her concern for Felix's whereabouts and the general mood of the place occupied her thoughts all the way from her house to the Comm Center. When she entered the main area, the mood was somber.

Even the cheery sunshine and gentle breeze outside did little to dispel the gloom of what had happened to a healthy portion of Star Light's residents.

As usual, the GGs occupied the middle area of the room. As Sabine approached, however, she could tell that while their position was unchanged, the women themselves were different now. No longer were they laughing and gossiping, their eyes darting around for their next prey, or person of interest. They sat quietly, barely speaking. Even their outfits were subdued, grays and beiges overtaking their usual riot of pastels and corals.

"Hello, girls," Sabine said, trying to adopt a tone of friendly support without giving a 'this-didn't affect-me' vibe.

The GGs looked up, their expressions tired.

"Hi, Sabine," said Topaz.

"Hi," Ginny chimed in.

"Hey," said Rebecca sullenly.

Grace merely waved a hand in a fatalistic way.

"Where's Helen?" Sabine asked, sitting down next to Topaz.

"Not sure. She's been kinda absent since this whole thing blew up. We're not sure why."

Grace shot Ginny a venomous look for speaking.

"We don't know exactly, but we have our suspicions. Just like everything about what's happened," she spat.

"Wait, what?" Sabine asked, totally confused.

"There are rumors that the scam came about because of that Thad character. You know, Helen's son," Rebecca said, leaning in close to Sabine and placing her hand on her forearm in that way that all women do when they are saying something salacious and savory all at once.

"You think that Helen's son had something to do with this?" Sabine sputtered.

"We can't prove it right now, but yes," Grace said, crossing her arms definitively. "I knew I shouldn't have listened to him!"

Now it was Sabine's turn to lean in conspiratorially.

"Do you think Helen knew about all this? That she was involved?"

She knew she shouldn't be asking these questions—shouldn't even be getting herself caught up in this kind of rumor-milling—but she couldn't help it.

It was all so exciting. And *wrong*! And so many other things.

"Why else has she gone AWOL?" Ginny hissed, accompanied by Grace's vigorous nodding.

But it didn't sit right with Sabine. Helen may have been vapid and a little lacking in personality, but she didn't seem the type to sneak off with the contents of her closest friends' bank accounts.

Something was wrong here. Very wrong.

"But there's hope," Topaz interjected, putting her hand on Grace's bony shoulder. Grace set her jaw, but Sabine detected the faintest lean into Topaz' touch.

Did even the stone-cold Grace Pickney need affection from time to time? For a moment, Sabine recalled holding Grace as she panicked the night of the show.

Yes, even the Grace Pickneys of the world need help sometimes...

""What kind of hope?" Sabine asked.

"Hope in the form of Felix Crenshaw," Topaz explained.

Surprise mixed with a nagging feeling of anxiety raced through Sabine. How was Felix involved in all this?

"He thinks he's fixed it. Made it all right. We're just

waiting to see. The banks have to catch up," Grace said tersely.

Topaz chimed in, "It could happen any time now. We just have to be patient. But I think he's gone and done it!"

The women traded back cautious statements about banking times and business days and phone call wait times while Sabine tuned them out.

Her mind thrummed like it was full of bees.

Sabine's memory swirled as she recalled Colin's last days before sickness forced his early retirement. She remembered how he ranted about being wronged by someone he never named. Sabine has asked him over and over to name this person. She had reasoned that perhaps it would help to talk about it. But Colin only wanted to rant. Sabine bit her lip as the bitter recollections resurfaced. They felt as fresh as if they had happened only yesterday.

Was that Felix back then? Was he to blame for Colin's business problems at the end?

And was Felix capable of cooking up a fancy scheme, taking advantage of people at Star Light—for whom he visibly held no love—then swooping in to restore it and become the hero?

None of it made any sense. Why would he do that? What would he have to gain by it?

But in her haste to be with Felix and in the dizzying moments when they had been intimate, she had been successful in pushing down these nagging doubts.

Sabine had always trusted her gut. Until now. Was that going to come back to haunt her?

Felix had been markedly absent since the incident on opening night. Especially considering their passionate clinch backstage. Was that suspicious too?

"Earth to Sabine! You okay?" Rebecca waved a hand in Sabine's face, jolting her back to the present.

"Uh... yes. Sorry. I just... have to get back to my garden," Sabine said lamely. She stood up to leave, tossing "I hope it all works out..." over her shoulder as she drifted away from their looks of confusion.

She had to get home. She had to think in the quiet of her own space.

More importantly, she had to speak to Felix.

About what, she didn't know.

Chapter 25

Confrontation Gone Wrong

"Felix, it's time we cleared the air..."

Too confrontational.

"Felix, I've really enjoyed our time together, but there's something I have to know about you..."

No.

"Felix, what's your deal, anyway? Are you a supervillain?"

Ugh.

Sabine sat down heavily on her sofa, her head in her hands. She'd been pacing so much, her heart rate was up and her palms were sweaty against her cheeks.

"No... I can't talk to him like that. Can I?"

All morning she had been practicing ways she could confront Felix. To finally clear the air between them. Or at least allay her fears that he was behind all the terrible things that had happened to her and around her.

Yes, that would make things all better, knowing he's totally blameless, one inner voice said reassuringly.

It was soon replaced by another, much more urgent voice.

161

But what if he's behind all of it and more? Isn't that why you're confronting him in the first place?

"Uggghhhh," she groaned, sinking deeper into confusion and despair.

She'd been up almost all night with this argument on loop in her head. Unfortunately, the light of day and several cups of coffee brought little to no clarity.

But she couldn't let it go. She couldn't go back to hanging out with Felix—doing whatever it was they were doing together—without having some sure footing. She had to know who he was. What he was capable of.

And what then? What if you find out the dastardly truth? That he's evil, after all?

The question gutted her.

If he was, she would have to leave Star Light. She would have to pack up and go. There was no way she could stay here. No way they could cross paths. No way she could continue to live near such despicable behavior.

Is that so bad? You thought about leaving not all that long ago...

"Uh! Stop!" Sabine yelled, tossing a throw pillow to the floor.

Then, without warning, she started laughing.

"I guess that's why they call them throw pillows."

The laughter helped lighten her mood a little but was quickly replaced by something else—a deep, void-like depression.

Here she was laughing by herself in her sunny living room. No one to share it with. Her immediate thought was whether Felix would find the whole situation amusing. Would he laugh with her or *at* her if he knew what agony she was in?

Funny how my first thoughts are of him, yet he might be the reason I have to go away.

What was her life now that she didn't have someone to share it with?

Would she ever share anything special with anyone again?

She thought she had already tackled these questions after Colin passed away, and yet here she was, practically at square one all over again.

Everything felt hopeless.

And did I just think about Felix before thinking about Colin? What does that say about me?

Standing, she glanced at her cell phone. It was, as usual, silent and devoid of messages. The most telling absence was that of Felix himself. He hadn't contacted her since that night of the crisis. She'd heard he'd been busy working whatever magic he could behind the scenes, but she hadn't seen or heard from him personally.

Yet another reason to be concerned.

Maybe he sensed I was on to him. After all, we were getting so close...

But, What had she done to give that away?

"Just go, Sabine," she said, trying to find the determination somewhere deep inside. "Just talk to him about it."

In less than a minute—before her resolve could crumble —she was out the door, stuffing a small purse with her keys, phone, and sunglasses.

She decided to walk, not only giving herself the exercise, but the time to rehearse what she was going to say. Trouble was she wasn't confident she would have the words by the time she reached his doorstep.

Just ask him. Just be honest. Just... be a friend first.

This last bit of self-advice helped spur her on as she walked along the path to his house.

As she approached his neatly maintained bungalow, she realized she had never been inside his home.

What will it be like?

She imagined neat rows of books and minimal furnishings. Soft colors and a closet with shirts hung just so. Despite her worries, she smiled to think of it. To wonder how Felix lived when no one was watching.

She found herself eager to go inside, to get to know him, to dispel these ugly worries once and for all.

At last, she reached his door and raised her hand to knock.

Indulging in a brief hesitation to summon her strength, she rapped her knuckles on the sun-warmed wood. Just a breath, though. She might lose her courage if she waited any longer.

An age seemed to pass by before the door finally opened. His car was in the driveway, so she was sure he must be home.

"Hello?"

A stranger opened the door. A young woman with brown hair tied back in a French braid. She wore no-nonsense khakis and a polo shirt. The sight of someone so unexpected robbed Sabine of whatever composure she'd managed.

"Oh! Hello! I'm... uh... looking for Felix Crenshaw?" Sabine stammered.

A slice of hot, sharp jealousy raced through Sabine's midsection. What was an attractive young woman doing here of all places?

The woman looked at Sabine with a sad smile.

"Oh? I'm so sorry. He's not here. I'm afraid he's still in the hospital."

Hospital? Still?

A void opened up in Sabine's middle—a familiar and awful feeling. One she had hoped never to feel again.

"Wha... why?"

The woman gasped.

"Oh! I thought you knew! I shouldn't have just blurted it out like that. Would you like to sit down?"

Sabine waved her hands. "No... uh... No. I just... I'm sorry, but what's going on?"

The woman sighed and regrouped.

"I'm Cassie—a social worker here at Star Light. Felix has been in the hospital for two days. I'm here to get some papers and other items the hospital needs. Are you a close friend?"

Sabine could barely hear Cassie's words. Instead, her head started ringing with a dull, persistent roar.

"I... uh... don't know... I... yes."

"Would you like some water or—" Before Cassie could finish, Sabine drifted off, leaving the young woman calling, "Hey! Where are you going? Do you need some help?" from behind her.

Cassie's pleas came in vain as Sabine floated away from Felix's house, unable to continue the conversation.

Felix was in trouble, and she hadn't known.

This man who had captivated her, aggravated her, tied up her mind and heart in knots was in trouble.

What was she going to do about it?

Chapter 26

Visiting Hours

"Sorry, the rules are the rules," the huffy hospital administrator said with a note of finality before walking away and leaving Sabine bereft.

"But, please? I..." Sabine's voice trailed off, a deep sense of sadness spreading through her guts like an oil spill.

She knew it was fruitless to argue. She had seen this type before—officious, unbending, callous. Just the right type of person to make sure a hospital isn't too caring or compassionate.

And one that stays on budget.

Sabine had clocked the sign listing the rules governing visitors to the ICU at Star Light's on-site medical facility, but she couldn't fathom that they'd be so strict about them.

"No one but relatives or spouses," the woman with the tightly cut hair and drab cardigan had told her.

Behind the front desk was a frosted glass wall, and just beyond she could make out the blurry shapes of beds and equipment—a complicated whir of dense devices and life-saving machines.

Somewhere, in all that, lay Felix.

Is he alone? Has anyone come to see him? If they have, are they treating him well?

Having lost her argument with the woman, Sabine stood in a state of numb inertia, unable to make a decision or even manage a coherent thought. That dreadful, low, needling buzzing rang through her temples, obliterating her ability to think straight.

Turning away, she shuffled towards a nearby plastic chair. Maybe sitting for a moment would help her focus.

"Excuse me? Did I hear you are trying to see Felix Crenshaw?"

Turning, Sabine saw a young male nurse watching her kindly. Decked in blue scrubs, he had a moonish, open face. Not handsome, but not unpleasant. With warm brown eyes and soft curls, he looked to be someone's grandson. He probably was. But at this moment, he seemed to be Sabine's only hope.

"Uh... yes," she replied.

"I'm Mitchell. I've been taking care of him."

Mitchell offered Sabine a handshake that was warm, comforting, and surprisingly strong. Mitchell's voice was soft, with just a hint of a lisp to it. Sabine could instantly see why Mitchell had chosen to be a nurse—compassion radiated from him.

"How is he?" Sabine asked, her words coming out in a rush.

Mitchell's face turned grave. "It's touch and go, I'm afraid. His heart has been through a lot."

Sabine's own heart constricted in her chest—a mixture of pain, sadness, and loss. She'd been through this all before.

"They won't..." Her words choked around the large knot in her throat. Clenching her hands in her lap, Sabine forced herself to keep going. "They won't let me see him."

Mitchell looked around conspiratorially.

"Screw that. We can bend the rules," he replied, motioning her behind the desk towards the door into the ICU.

"But what about..."

"Muriel? Forget about her. She's gone to lunch and won't be back for several hours. You know—she's got 'meetings.'" Mitchell put air quotes around the word, rolling his eyes. "She's not what we could call hands-on—until she can ruin some poor visitor's day. She loves doing that."

Within seconds, Sabine was through the frosted door and into a small locker room-type area. Mitchell instructed her to put on a paper gown, booties, mask, gloves, and cap.

"The cap will hide your face," he winked. "From Muriel."

"Why are you helping me out? Not that I don't appreciate it, I do..." Sabine gushed as she wriggled her fingers into the rubber gloves, trying and failing to keep her emotions in check.

Mitchell hesitated before answering.

"Because you're the only one that's come to see him," he said at last. A crashing wave of sadness washed over Sabine, her heart and lungs locking up for what seemed like an age.

Did he really have no one? No one on this Earth who cared enough to visit? Had he alienated them all? Or had his bad deeds caught up to him at the worst possible moment?

Somehow, these questions didn't faze her. She still had to see him. Be there for him. She couldn't fathom why, given the creeping suspicion that he was the person she had feared all along.

Freezing her expression into a poker face behind her paper mask, she followed Mitchell out of the dressing area and into the labyrinth of beds, curtains, and cordoned areas of the ICU.

All around her were the sounds of beeps, and blips, and hisses of breathing machines—an eerie chorus of the business of life.

Each curtained area contained someone in deep distress. Sabine counted at least five along the passage. Shapeless forms under sheets, tubes, and monitors pouring from under the crisp whiteness of the bleached bed linens.

At last they came to the end bay—a corner suite with a window. Weak sunlight filtered through tinted windows, meekly peeking in as if it knew it should tread carefully.

At first, Sabine couldn't see Felix. There was a still form on the bed. There was the tenting of his toes, but the rest of him was obscured by a man in a lab coat.

Mitchell stopped and whispered, "That's Dr. Watkins. He's the cardiologist. He's the best."

At his words, Dr. Watkins turned, giving them both a warm smile. It eased Sabine's frayed nerves, if only slightly. The man gave off an air of quiet confidence.

With reddish hair and sparkling green eyes, his youthful energy belied his age. He might have been in his sixties, if Sabine had to guess. Close to her own age, even, but worlds apart. He merely worked here while others of their age group called it home.

"Ah, pardon me," Dr. Watkins said genially. "I didn't know Felix was expecting anyone. How do you do?" He didn't extend his hand as per ICU protocol, but he did give a friendly nod.

"Nice to meet you. I'm Sabine. Uh... could you—?"

She didn't know how to ask the question. She didn't even know what question she wanted to ask. There were far too many crowding her brain.

Fortunately, Dr. Watkins anticipated her distress and took control of the conversation.

But first, he led her away from Felix's bedside, guiding her to two plastic chairs in the corner of the room. Mitchell gave Sabine one last look of kindness and slipped away, no doubt to attend to his other patients.

"So." Dr. Watkins crossed his legs, resting his hands on his knee. "Mr. Crenshaw is in a coma. An induced one, until we can get his rhythms stable."

"But what...?"

"He didn't have a heart attack, per se, but something damn near as dangerous. He had a bubble in his aorta. That kind of thing is quite freakish, actually. Impossible to predict or prevent. He must have been dealing with something stressful because the bubble decided to rear its ugly head and burst on him in the worst possible part of his heart. So, here he is, and I'm doing my best to get him out of the woods. But first, we have to make sure his heart is strong enough to get better."

"And will it?" Sabine asked, hot tears stinging her eyelids.

"In theory, yes. Between you and I?" He leaned forward, an encouraging glint in his eyes. "Felix is as healthy as a horse. Fitter than I am, in fact. This was just a genetic predisposition that has really knocked him down."

For a moment, silence lingered between them, Dr. Watkins giving it a professional pause while Sabine processed and formed her next question.

"Will... will he live?"

A crushing weight descended on her just asking the question. Was she ready to accept his answer, no matter what?

The professional mask slipped just a little before he replied. "Hard to say. That's why I'm glad you're here."

He stood up and squeezed her shoulder. "I have to make rounds, but please let me know if you have any more questions. I'll do my very best by him."

Sabine could only nod as he left the room.

For several moments, she could do nothing but stare at Felix's motionless form on the bed.

He lay on his back, his head propped on two pillows. A nasal cannula fed him oxygen, and various tubes and patches disappeared under the sheet. No doubt connected to vital parts of his body.

His body.

Sabine's mind raced through their times together—the glisten of his skin, the tautness of his muscles.

His hair lay limp against the bleached white pillow, and his silver beard was starting to grow unruly from not being kept up.

Summoning her courage, she stood and crept to his bedside, a curious blend of terror and determination coursing through her.

He lay still as stone. So still that Sabine made herself watch the minute rising of his chest as the machines forced air into him. Soft beeps and whistles drummed out a steady rhythm. A hateful noise Sabine knew all too well.

This is the worst kind of deja vu.

"Hello," she forced herself to say, her voice scratchy and raw.

She tried again.

"Hello, Felix. It's Sabine. I..."

She didn't know what to say. Didn't know if he could hear her. Despair threatened to overwhelm her. She bit the inside of her cheek to stop herself from collapsing in tears.

Get yourself together, she rebuked. *Felix needs you.*

She took his hand in hers. It was cool and dry—almost chapped. An unbidden mental note came into her brain to bring moisturizer next time. And perhaps a razor. Just for the edges. She knew he'd like that. If they'd let her, that is. Maybe even a book to read to him. And some flowers.

The list was comforting. Something to grasp. Something to do. Something to help.

Then and there, she calcified her fear and anxiety into action—resolving to be there for Felix.

No matter what he might have done, he didn't deserve to be left alone now.

And she would be the one to help.

"I'll be back," she whispered, lifting his hand to her lips for a quick kiss. "Don't go anywhere."

Turning, Sabine left the room, determined to be back within the hour. And if anybody tried to stop her?

Well, Muriel would just have to deal with it.

Chapter 27

A Blur of Days

"Hon? Psst, hon? Come on, honey, you gotta wake up."

Sabine blinked and immediately snapped to alertness. *How long have I been out? What's happened?*

Sitting up in the hard plastic chair, her neck and shoulders throbbed. Clearly she'd slept in an awkward position, but for how long?

Disoriented and embarrassed, her mood shifted slightly when she discovered who had woken her.

It was Mitchell, his hand on her shoulder, kind eyes trained on her face.

"Just letting you know that I'm ending my shift and that there's a rumor Muriel is on the prowl. You might want to get out of here for a bit. I promise, she'll be gone soon—I hear she's going on vacation *again*."

Mitchell winked at Sabine with a sly grin on his face.

Ever since Sabine had taken up post next to Felix' bed, Mitchell had been her watchdog, letting her know when Muriel was near and when she could return. He'd been right about that woman. Muriel was an inconsistent supervisor, and her visits were never long. Even so, Sabine wanted to avoid her at all costs.

At the same time, she never wanted to be away from Felix. What if he woke up? What if he needed her? The doctors all assured her that they were in control of his coma—it was necessary for his heart to heal and for him to regain his strength, but still, she knew stranger things had happened, and she wanted to be there when he opened his eyes.

It didn't make any sense given what she thought about the man and what he might have done his whole life. But when she was away from him—either to grab a shower or sleep a few hours in her own bed, she felt like ants were crawling through her insides.

Her sleep was terrible, and the only peace she could get was by his side. Bags formed under her eyes, and her clothes drooped off of her. She knew she was losing weight, but she was determined to see this through.

If Felix woke up and Sabine found out she had been right all along, then she'd have to rethink her plans. But for now, she was his only advocate. His only... friend?

She wasn't sure what term applied to her, but that was a question for another time.

"Thanks, Mitchell. You're a doll," Sabine said, rubbing her eyes and fetching her purse. "There's no way—?" she began to say.

Mitchell raised a reassuring hand.

"There's no way he's going to wake up when you're gone. We've been over this, honey. When they are ready to wake him, I'll be sure to let you know. Muriel or no Muriel."

Sabine rested her hand on his and squeezed. She was so grateful for this man.

"Okay. I'll get out of here. But only for a little bit."

"Atta girl. See you in a few."

By now, Sabine had practically memorized the shift change schedule in the ICU and would return when Mitchell clocked back in—at least twelve hours from now. It was daunting but had to be done. Muriel was due at any moment.

After gathering her things, she gave one last look at Felix. His beard was trimmed and the edges cleaned thanks to her efforts, and his hair looked more presentable. Sabine had washed him and combed his hair, certain he would have wanted to look decent no matter what state he was in. The man's fastidious nature was well known.

"I'll be back soon," she whispered, giving his long fingers a slight squeeze.

Then she left, walking the now familiar forty-five steps from his room to the lobby.

She moved as if underwater, like her whole body was submerged in glue. She couldn't recall ever being this tired. A shower and a proper nap would do her good. She shoved thoughts of leaving Felix to the side of her brain, trying to focus only on the present.

Stepping out of the ICU doors, she was confronted with something wholly unexpected.

The GGs.

They were dressed in a panoply of bright colors and textures, all squealing as Sabine appeared. They clutched flowers, improbably shiny balloons, and even a giant turquoise teddy bear. It was like stepping into a bag of candy. Sabine instantly wanted to retreat to the quiet of Felix' room.

"There she is! We've caught you red-handed!" Grace said, somewhere between a purr and a screech. It set

Sabine's teeth on edge and made the front desk clerk look at them with disdain. But nobody dared discipline Grace Pickney—especially not the staff at Star Light. Not the smart ones, anyway.

"Uhh... what are you all doing here?" Sabine asked, wary as she was weary.

The GGs flicked their eyes at Sabine, then back to each other, and then back to Sabine—at once assessing and reassessing how they felt about finding her here. More for the gossip it would create than any real concern they might feel for her.

It is all so confusing—how they care about me and yet use me for amusement at the same time, Sabine realized. She didn't know how to feel about it at all.

"We are here," Grace began, "to show our thanks to Felix, who has somehow managed to restore our accounts! Without him, I don't know *what* we would have done."

Sabine looked around at them. Only Helen was subdued, as if she was being punished somehow. Had her son really had something to do with this? What had Felix discovered? Or, more importantly... what had Felix done?

Sabine hated that she couldn't get those nagging thoughts out of her head.

"Oh, that's so great..." Sabine said evenly, wanting this whole conversation to end. She craved a hot shower and her own bed now more than ever. The colors, the smell of the GGs collective perfume, and their chatter were too much for her waterlogged brain and exhausted body.

"You've seen better days. Do you live here?" Topaz asked, her eyes flicking up and down, taking in Sabine's rumpled sweatpants and raggedy hoodie. Her hair was pulled back in a rough ponytail.

Sabine squirmed under their gaze. She didn't want to

confess how much time she had spent at the ICU in the past two weeks. How her life had been consumed by caring for Felix. But surely they already knew? Surely they had clocked her absence around the Comm or that they hadn't seen her anywhere on the grounds.

"Yeah, I've been... just here for him. He doesn't have family nearby, so..."

Grace laid a hand on Sabine's upper arm, an odd blend of pity and genuine sympathy on her face.

"We get it, honey. We really do."

Sabine had the distinct impression that they really didn't. That Grace wanted more from Sabine—that she wanted her to confess why she was there and had spent most of her waking hours there. But Sabine couldn't answer that for herself—let alone anyone else. She just wanted to get home.

"Thanks. Uh, I'm not sure if you can actually visit him —the rules are pretty strict around here, but—"

Grace cut her off.

"I know the right people," she said, and swept past Sabine with one more squeeze to her arm.

The others followed, their balloons and flowers rustling and crinkling.

They were about to open the door leading into the inner sanctum of the ICU when a figure stopped them.

"Ladies, ladies! What a breath of fresh air you are!" Dr. Watkins cooed, his eyes glinting. Sabine was grateful an adult had stepped into the room. And one, she suspected, who was adept at handling tricky customers.

Grace wriggled under the weight of his attention, appreciative of his tone, stature, good looks, and obvious flattery.

"Hello, Dr...?"

"Watkins. Dr. Watkins. I'm the chief cardiologist here at Star Light, and I am very glad to see you bringing cheer to our patients. May I ask who it is you are here to see?"

Sidling up to him and laying a perfectly manicured paw on his white coat, Grace said, "Felix Crenshaw. He's a darling, you know."

Sabine couldn't be certain, but she thought she saw Dr. Watkins clench his jaw in irritation. She was thinking the same thing:

Where have you been this whole time? Why the sudden show of love now?

"Ah, yes. One of my star patients," Dr. Watkins said, his voice smooth as caramel.

"Of course! He's a star to us too!" Grace replied, moving past the doctor to the door.

He stepped to the side, blocking her path with an elegance that Sabine thought was masterful.

"Ladies... I'm flattered on Felix' behalf that you are here to see him, but I'm afraid I can't let you back there. It's a highly delicate situation and we have a lot of other compromised patients—"

Grace turned cold.

"I'm sure you understand my need to get back there and my place on the board of this hospital, Doctor," Grace said, curling the 'r' of his title like a whip. Grace could turn from cat to panther in an instant.

"I understand that, and I'm ever so thankful for that, but Felix is about to undergo a procedure, and believe me, you don't want to be there when we insert the needle."

The GGs stopped. Grace turned an odd shade of green for a moment.

"What... what kind of needle?"

"Well, it will go directly into his chest. It's about yea long..."

Grace backed away at his words, her obvious phobia of such things on full display.

"I understand. Thank you for sparing us that. We can come back another time."

Dr. Watkins beamed a 1,000-watt smile. Sabine stood in awe of his diplomacy.

"Of course. And if this goes well, he'll be awake and ready to receive your lovely gifts. Now, if I could speak to Miss Wilcox alone..." His eyes trailed to Sabine, and the GGs gave her another look of hawkish curiosity and filed out, their loud presents still in their arms.

Sabine's anxiety bloomed, her hands instantly clenched, and her heart raced. She stood stone still, waiting for the last of the GGs to make their exit.

Dr. Watkins turned to her, a look of triumph mixed with seriousness on his face.

"They're *something*, aren't they?" The doctor must have seen the terror on her face, because he softened and lowered his tone. "Let's find somewhere more private to chat."

Though she barely knew this man, something about his confidence and the mischievous gleam in his eye told her to trust him. She nodded in consent.

He led her to a small anteroom and sat her on a chair while he took the opposite. There was an air about him that managed to be both kind and serious.

"I wasn't lying to those women just now. We do want to try something. A small procedure that will insert a special gauge into his heart and allow us to monitor him. It may also allow us to ensure this never happens again. We think he's healthy enough to handle it. And, if it goes well, we can wake him up."

Sabine hugged herself, trying to keep calm.

"But...? I feel there's a catch here."

Dr. Watkins nodded. "There's always a catch with these things. He could get an infection. His heart could go into an abnormal rhythm that we can't control. A number of things could occur, but given his current state, the chances of anything like that are very, very minimal."

"How minimal?"

"Legally, I can't tell you zero, but pretty close to it."

Somehow, Sabine couldn't let herself be comforted by this. And yet, she wanted to feel Felix's eyes on her once more. Wanted to see him smile. That was worth it, right?

Or am I being selfish?

Dr. Watkins took her hands in his.

"I promise I'll do everything I can for him."

Sabine nodded, her throat too choked to say anything resembling words.

Dr. Watkins stood and stretched. "Okay then. I have to prepare for this. We'll do it first thing tomorrow morning. Did you want to leave now or...?"

"I'll go and see him again, if you don't mind," she said, her determination returning to her. She turned to go. "Oh!" Sabine cringed, catching herself mid-step. "What about Muriel?"

Dr. Watkins snorted. "Don't you worry about her. She answers to me. If she gives you guff, tell her I said you could be there."

Relief flooded Sabine. From the way he viewed the GGs to the way he gave her the honest truth about Felix's condition, she was more than reassured. In fact, she could have kissed him, she was so grateful. Instead, she mumbled a thanks and hurried back to Felix's room.

The afternoon shadows were fading, their surrender to the coming evening already well advanced.

Felix was every bit as still as when she'd just left him, his breathing regular, the machines carrying on their dull refrain. Some vague part of her had imagined he might be different somehow. Better. More vital.

She took her seat beside him, the fatigue of earlier crawling at the edges of her awareness. But she would not give in to it.

Taking his hand, she looked at him—really looked— mapped the contours of his face, the peaks and valleys of his nose, and the curve of his lips. Her eyes swooped over the plunge of his hair off his forehead, the peak of his shoulders emerging from the crisp white sheets.

Her heart ached. Her lungs felt solid with worry and concern.

Why? What has this man done to me? Why do I care about him so much?

"Oh, Felix…" she sighed, her head dropping to her chest. Waves of emotion buffeted against her tired heart and body, and she surrendered to the feeling she had pushed away for so long.

"I love you," she whispered, snapping her head up as she said it. In an instant she'd opened Pandora's box. She couldn't unsay it. Even if he hadn't heard her—and it was likely he hadn't—it was out there now. A living thing. A phantom writ large by being spoken into existence.

She loved him.

No matter what he was. No matter who he had been. He made her want to live life more fully and enjoy all that was left for her. Be happy in someone's eyes, arms, and heart.

And that someone was Felix.

Against all odds, it was him.

He had to live.

She knew it like she knew she had to breathe.

Her head began to dip once more, the rollercoaster of the past few minutes overloading her fragile state.

With her hand still in his, she fell asleep as evening's shadows crossed into the room.

<h1 style="text-align:center">Chapter 28</h1>

<h2 style="text-align:center">Dawn Arrives</h2>

"Think she'll ever wake up? Anyone taking bets?"

These questions floated through the haze of Sabine's brain, and, in an instant, she jolted awake. It was becoming a habit that she didn't much prefer, but recently her life had taken such an odd turn, and living in the ICU was fast becoming almost normal.

"What? How long was I...?" Sabine said, her words slightly slurred and a little too loud.

She rubbed at her eyes, trying to adjust to the harsh morning light. Her neck ached horribly, and her clothes clung like an unpleasant second skin.

She turned towards the source of the voice, realizing that she'd been asleep far longer than she'd intended. And who had moved her to this side of the room? What was going on?

In an instant, all her questions turned into amazement, her confusion morphing with lightning speed into joyful surprise.

"Morning, Sunshine," said a voice, and she had to blink twice to check if she wasn't in a dream.

183

Felix Crenshaw sat looking at her. He was propped up, his bed at an angle. Most of the tubes that had surrounded him for so long were missing, and though he looked tired and slightly pale, his eyes sparkled with some of their old light. His smile was aimed directly at her. Her heart clenched at the sight.

"Felix! Is that really you? Are you... awake?"

Sabine unfolded herself from her chair and moved towards him. Mitchell stood on the other side of Felix, his face one huge grin.

"Guess I should have been quicker with that bet," Mitchell quipped.

"Guess so," Felix said. His voice was raspy with disuse, but he was *talking*.

He's awake. That's all that matters.

In three steps, she was at his side, her hand in his. Sabine was acutely aware she hadn't showered, that her hair was probably a frightful mess, and that she desperately needed to brush her teeth. But she was willing to risk anything just to be near him. To prove that he was awake and that his smile was real and not a figment of her exhausted imagination.

"Yes, it's really me, to answer your question," Felix rasped. "I'm back. Most of me, I think."

She played with his fingers, checking to see if this was all a dream. They were warm and alive—a far cry from the cold digits she'd held for so many days on end.

"But how?"

Felix looked to Mitchell, his energy low. Mitchell was happy to oblige.

"Dr. Watkins, to put it simply. The man is a miracle worker," the young man reported.

"Was I asleep the whole time?" Sabine asked, her

embarrassment settling on her like a shawl. How could she have missed something so monumental?

"Yes, and that's the best way, actually. It was nice and quiet for the doc to do his work. You see, we moved you," Mitchell said, his eyes glinting playfully.

"That's why I was in the corner?"

"Believe me, if you saw the size of the needle, you'd rush over there," Mitchell quipped. "So, I'm sorry I broke my promise about making sure you were there when he woke up. This really is the best way."

Sabine shook her head, trying to dislodge the mental picture that sprang to mind. Maybe it was good she hadn't been awake to see the procedure that had worked such wonders.

"Hey, it doesn't matter," Felix said, his smile dimming. He was struggling to stay awake, and Sabine pulled up a chair so he wouldn't have to strain to see her.

Mitchell sensed the change in the temperature and headed towards the exit.

"I'll give you a few minutes, and then I'll come back. Felix will probably need his beauty sleep soon. And Sabine, you can get that shower you were trying for yesterday. We need you fresh and spry for this next phase. Felix, I'll be back soon. Try not to get into any trouble while I'm gone."

Mitchell winked at them and disappeared. Sabine turned back to Felix, amazed to see his grey-blue eyes looking at her. She could tell he was fading, but he worked hard to stay with her.

"I'm so happy you are awake. I—" She couldn't find the next words to say—so many thoughts crowded her head, and she lacked the precision to choose the right ones to fit this impossibly big moment.

Luckily, Felix sensed her distress and spoke up.

"I heard you. The whole time I was in a coma. I could hear your voice talking to me. I can't tell you how comforting that was."

His hand gave a slight squeeze, and his eyelids started to droop, his face growing slack.

An explosion of light flooded Sabine's chest, mixed with the panic of this moment already becoming the past.

She finally knew what to say.

"I meant every word," she said simply, her hand clenched firmly in his, determined never to let it go.

Chapter 29

Doctor's Orders

"She's gone, right?" Felix asked, his eyes darting towards the door. Mitchell stood near, his hands on his hips, wearing a look of slight disapproval.

"Yes, she's gone for the night. Probably about to sleep the sleep of the damned after taking care of you all day," Mitchell said teasingly. "What that woman does for you..."

Felix gritted his teeth and swung his legs out of the bed. He hated their sluggish weight but knew he had to get stronger, had to get his body moving again. He was determined to get back to his old self.

"Why do you think I want her gone? So she doesn't have to worry about one more thing!" Felix said, his voice barely contained. He liked Mitchell and could see how relaxed he made Sabine, even with all the daily indignities of ICU life, but sometimes Felix wished he would keep his opinions to himself.

"Because you're vain and don't like looking weak," Mitchell retorted, pulling the sheet from Felix's legs so he wouldn't get tangled.

"No. Wrong," Felix said, slowly swinging each leg as

187

they hung from the side of the bed. The sensation of them moving, while difficult, felt good. The act of stretching his muscles was the right mix of sore and satisfying. "I'm trying to get stronger so she doesn't have to be a nursemaid. So I can come home and be myself again. And to give her a damn break!"

Mitchell made a little tsk noise and took a wide stance in front of Felix. He opened his arms, and Felix rested himself into the young man's torso. Together, they lifted upwards, and Felix managed to pull into a standing position.

"Alright, I'll allow it this time," Mitchell said, his smile playful as he helped Felix take some tentative steps. "If only because I can tell you are getting stronger. And because Sabine is my girl."

"Stronger, huh? You think so?" Felix asked, genuinely curious. For him, each day he got out of bed was just as hard as the day before. Every time he worked on his strength, he felt it was a game of inches. If that.

Mitchell nodded. "I do. Every day."

Felix chose to believe him. He realized he didn't have much choice, and to not believe would be far too bleak.

Together they began their glacial routine of moving across Felix's hospital room. As if locked in a middle school slow dance, the two men made an arduous journey towards the window. Night had fallen, and despite his exertion and frustration, Felix could see the twinkling lights of Star Light in the darkness beyond the curtains.

Felix did most of the work. Mitchell held him up and steadied him when he wavered, but Felix was determined to do it on his own. Determined to make his legs move with the effortlessness he was used to. Felix was no slouch, and he had decided that no mere freak heart condition would stop him now.

But he couldn't escape the notion that his legs were giving out, could feel his strength sapping away. When, at long last, they reached the window, Felix called for a time out. Mitchell lowered him into a chair close by, and Felix tried to take deep, long breaths, but his anger kept stopping him.

"Dammit!" He exclaimed, hitting the armrest. "I hate this."

Self-pity was the last thing he wanted to give in to, but it welled up in his chest in a jagged, awful wave. He wasn't used to these feelings. He didn't have the tools to fight them off.

Mitchell knelt down in front of him, a small crack of his knees making him wince.

"Hey. Look at me. Look at me, Felix Crenshaw."

Felix forced himself to look at the young man, his breath rapid.

"I see what you are doing, and I'm here to support you. And know this: you are getting better. Every day. I can see it and so should you."

Felix let his guard down. Just a little.

"But... can she?"

Mitchell nodded slowly.

"Yes. She can. Even if she doesn't know it yet. Now, get up, and let's get you back across this room."

Felix squared his jaw and dug deep.

He was going to get there. Somehow.

Chapter 30

Road to Recovery and Beyond

"Oh, what a day! Eventually everyone grows up and leaves me," Mitchell said, play-acting being sad. He waved his hands over his eyes, making a big show of things.

Sabine laughed while Felix grimaced.

"Stop it, it's time!" Felix growled, though everyone could tell he was only pretending to be annoyed.

Mitchell immediately dropped his act.

"You bet your ass it's time. I'll be glad to see the back of ya!"

"Ha! That's only because you had to wash it more than a few times," Felix snapped back, and the nurse and his patient shared a laugh. Sabine stood nearby, smiling and laughing along with them, amazed that this day had finally come.

Two weeks had passed since Dr. Watkins worked his magic, and Felix was building strength every day. He no longer needed to be in the ICU—or even a hospital. It would be a while before he was out and about again, but being home and comfortable was what the doctor ordered.

And everyone was ready for it. Though Sabine would miss seeing Mitchell every day.

"I promise we'll stay in touch," she said, a tiny swell of melancholy rising through her.

"You better. Who else will I complain to about Muriel?" Mitchell's devilish grin lit up the room, and a mild twinge caught Sabine in the chest. She had never been good at goodbyes.

"I'm sure you'll find someone else to pamper. You'll forget all about us," Sabine said as she zipped up Felix's bag.

"Never! And not people as cute as the two of you. Now, before I get all misty, let me get the discharge papers. Be back in a tic," Mitchell said, winking and leaving the room.

Felix and Sabine looked at each other. Felix from his wheelchair, and she from her spot by the bed. "Your house is all ready. I checked it this morning. It's been scrubbed, and fresh sheets are on the bed, and there are groceries and everything. It's like you've never been away," Sabine said, reassuringly.

Felix nodded. He was wearing his own clothes now, though they hung on him a little looser after losing some weight over the past few weeks. His tan had also faded, but his eyes sparkled with excitement at getting out of the ICU at last.

"Thank you for arranging all that. I owe you..."

"Oh please," she snapped, waving her hand. "I'd like to think you'd do the same for me."

The statement hung in the air—their obligations to each other awkwardly naked for a moment.

What is my obligation to this man? And what is he to me? And what about...

"Hey, Sabine? You still here?"

Felix waved his hand, playfully trying to get Sabine's

attention. She shook her head, annoyed at herself for getting distracted.

With Felix finally leaving the hospital, all the nagging thoughts and questions about Felix's past and history came rushing back to her. She could no longer put them off, no longer procrastinate. She had to confront them. It was long overdue to find out who this man—a man she now had intense feelings for—really was.

"Sorry! I just..."

"Look, I know I've been a huge pain in the ass. But you don't need to care for me anymore. I can get help at home. I can have aides come in. And I'm getting stronger every day. It'll only be for a while and then I'll be up to my old tricks again."

Now it was time for Sabine to wave at him.

"No! I said I'd help you, and I mean it. You think I'm going to abandon you now that you're out? I need some return on my investment here!"

The joke landed with a thud between them, but Felix did his best to give her a weak smile.

"Sabine. I don't want a nursemaid. I want..."

He drifted off, unable or unwilling to complete the sentence.

Neither of us knows what we want, she mused. *Or what we are to each other*.

The hospital stay had been a reprieve, a limbo for them both. Now, some hard truths would have to be faced. But how?

"I am okay staying with you—or at least being there when you need me until you feel strong enough—"

Felix cut her off. "Move in with me until I'm better, and then I'll move in with you."

The air pressed right out of her lungs.

Did he just... propose moving in together?

Sabine didn't know whether to be flattered, elated, or scandalized. How presumptuous of him! To come into her space! To be in her house... she wasn't sure what her face was expressing, since she herself didn't know what she was even feeling.

Felix must have sensed the change and cocked an eyebrow.

"What? I have my motives, you know. For starters, your view is better."

A weak laugh escaped her, and she looked at the floor. She felt ragged around the edges—unsure how to respond, react, or feel about this man that flipped her whole world upside down.

Again.

Is he serious? Does he want to start a life together? Have we already done so? Am I suddenly trapped with a man I barely know?

Thoughts of Colin raced into her mind. She had to find out what Felix had been in his past life. Those questions grasped at her—pushed their way to the forefront of her mind, unwilling to be ignored.

She heard footsteps approaching—Mitchell was near. Felix looked at her expectantly.

"Let's get you home first and focus on one day at a time, okay?" Sabine said, though she wasn't sure she said it convincingly.

He seemed to sense her confusion and distress and wore an easygoing smile.

Sabine forced one in return, though she wasn't sure if she'd sold it.

Luckily, Mitchell breezed in a moment later, a sheaf of papers in his hand.

"Alright, kids. Time to get sprung!"

He grabbed the handles of Felix's wheelchair and pushed him from the room.

"Say goodbye to this place, Felix! I don't want to see you in here ever again!"

They were out the door, Sabine trailing behind.

Felix called out, "Sayonara, room! Hope the next sucker in there is just as lucky as I am!"

Mitchell laughed, and Sabine trailed the two men as they made their way down the hallway, making small talk. She carried the bags and counted the steps one last time.

45–44–43...

Each step led to wherever life was taking her next.

Chapter 31

Coming Home

"Do you want anything else?" Sabine asked, drying her hands on the kitchen towel. She surveyed the room. The kitchen was clean, the dishes were done, and Felix had finished lunch. His meds had been given, and the afternoon seemed bright with possibility—the quiet, slow-moving kind.

"I'm fine. Maybe a walk would be nice, though," Felix said, rising out of his armchair.

Sabine threw the towel down and headed across from the kitchen to the living room, where Felix sat. She moved quickly, instantly worried.

"I'm fine, I'm fine. Stop fussing, Grandma!" Felix snarled.

Sabine stopped in her tracks, a little stung. She couldn't tell if he was joking or if he was actually angry she'd been so quick to race towards him.

"I'm sorry, I just..."

Felix was standing now, his linen pants slightly wrinkled and his t-shirt hanging oddly off his shoulders. Though thinner, he still looked handsome. Slowly gaining back the weight he had lost, but his movements were slower, more deliberate.

He sighed and looked at her.

"Sabine. I have to get moving. I'm going crazy in this house. And I know you worry, but—"

"I am just being cautious, that's all," she replied, annoyed that her voice sounded cloying, insistent.

Felix held out a hand, the other steadying his body against the recliner. He was standing on his own two feet, and though he didn't look like he was going to run a marathon anytime soon, Sabine had to admit that he was getting stronger all the time. She was glad to see it, but still so worried that if they moved too fast, if they pushed too hard too soon, he would relapse.

And it was too much to expect that Dr. Watkins could work a second miracle.

"Come here." Felix offered his hand and she took it, their palms resting perfectly together. "I know you mean well, but I'm not going to break. I know my own body, and I need to move it. And you're here. I won't do anything to risk you being my nursemaid again."

Roguish charm played over his lips as he smiled at her. Those gray eyes danced. Maybe they didn't have their usual sparkle, but Sabine could see that their full light was slowly returning. Her anxiety abated, replaced by a warm flutter in the middle of her chest.

"Well, I'm still kinda your nursemaid," Sabine said. "And your cleaning lady, and your cook, and your..." She trailed off, not sure where she wanted to go with her little joke.

Just as she'd lived at the ICU, she now basically lived at Felix's—sleeping in his guest room so as not to disturb him—

and ensuring he was fed, clean, and medicated as per doctor's orders.

Soon this period would end, just as his ICU stay had ended, and they would have to face whatever was next.

Which was... she didn't know.

"You are so many things to me," Felix replied, capping off her effort at being funny with something that was touching and real. The flutter in her chest intensified.

He squeezed her hand and leaned in to kiss her cheek. She let him, eager to smell his skin, to feel the aura of his warmth.

As he came close, he whispered in her ear.

"Do you really want to be my nursemaid? You know, I've been an awfully bad patient."

He pulled away, and Sabine's insides flip-flopped. His close proximity had awakened the magnetic pull of their bodies. The feelings of desire and closeness that they had last shared in the dusty backstage of the theatre. She hadn't allowed herself to think of those things since his hospital stay had begun; his care and mere survival had been so consuming.

Now, however, they all came rushing back, and her whole body tingled with the thrill of wanting him.

Her brain, however, intervened.

She pulled away.

"Felix! I can't even think of such things. You're still recovering. You need to rest. You need—"

His arm snaked around her waist, pulling her close with a strength that surprised her.

"You, Sabine," he said, gazing into her eyes. "I need you. Your body. Your beautiful skin. The feel of you. The moan in your voice."

Her protestations grew weaker, but still she tried to halt his advances.

"Felix... you need to be careful. I don't want to—"

He stopped her mouth with a kiss—long and passionate, their bodies melting into one another. All her reservations fell away. With a kiss that powerful, maybe he was strong enough for... *more?*

He drew back, and she instantly regretted the thought.

"Are you okay? Do you need to sit down?" she asked, her anxiety returning full force.

He put a finger to her lips.

"Shhh, I'm fine. I just wanted to tell you that I do have something wrong with me."

"What?" she choked.

"Something is happening... down there."

He flicked his eyes downward, and she felt the pressing bulge in her hip. She searched his face, and he instantly began to smile—devilish and unmistakably alluring.

She wanted to slap him.

"You are a *bad* patient, Felix Crenshaw. I ought to report you to the doctor."

"And I think," he replied, pulling her close again, "that you need to work on your bedside manner. I know you nurses can work wonders, and I've seen what you can do with a condition like mine. Won't you help me, nurse? *Please?*"

He leaned into her neck as he spoke, his breath hot on her skin. Flames of passion rose up in her once more, banishing the worries.

"I guess I could find some ways to help you..." she breathed, knowing she was doing a poor imitation but not caring. She just wanted him.

He gave a small sound of victory as he began to kiss her

neck, his hands fanning out over her back, sliding inside her blouse to touch her skin. Sabine gasped at the physical contact. She didn't realize how thirsty she had been for his skin, his touch, and his scent.

Now that she had them, she felt drunk.

Intoxicated by him.

A small voice cautioned her to take things slow, to be careful for his sake.

Felix must have sensed it too, for they moved as if trapped in molasses, a tender slowness to their kisses and caresses.

Without speaking, they broke away, their hands finding each other, the fingers intertwined.

Together, they crossed the living room, heading to Felix's spare but tasteful bedroom—the bed turned down with freshly laundered sheets.

Decadent afternoon sunlight shone hazily through the gauzy dark grey curtains, softening every corner and edge.

They stopped at the side of the bed and, for a moment, merely looked at each other, both hands clasped.

"I missed you," Felix said, his voice a husky whisper.

"And I missed you too. Are you sure about this?"

He nodded once, his eyes clear. "Completely. Let's just take it slow."

"And you'll stop if you need to."

"Scout's honor," he replied. "But I don't think I'll have to."

He winked and let go of her hands, bringing them up to cradle his face.

She let herself be kissed, his lips warm and inviting. Deep, slow kisses chased each other as her fingers danced through his hair.

Half kissing, half touching, they undressed with care;

movements graceful and deliberate, the revealing of skin a delight to be savored.

Soon, they stood naked together, desire and wonder binding them both.

It felt ritualistic, a dance to be enjoyed and honored. A reunion of souls.

Without speaking, they sank to the bed, their kisses bringing them together and apart—each break only to smile at the other—an act of appreciation.

"Lie back," Sabine instructed, a surge of power and energy running through her. She wanted to care for him in a new way now—nurture and restore his manhood, his sexual self. She had nursed him in so many other ways, she hadn't realized this was something else she could do.

It filled her with optimism and a newly charged sense of desire. That her body could restore his.

He lay back, his head framed by the soft gray sheets, his eyes shining with anticipation.

The muscles of his chest still rippled, the valleys and peaks of his arms apparent as he pulled her towards him.

His manhood rose and swelled against her and she could feel her own body respond with readiness.

And though passion swelled within her, she didn't mind taking her time. The need to simply be present blanketed them both, and she cherished it.

Sabine straddled Felix's hips, leaned down, and kissed him. Deep and sensually, pushing his head back into the pillow.

Then, as if surfacing for air, she pulled back, sitting tall. Taking both his hands in hers, she gave him a look of invitation and power. A look that told him she was in charge.

He smiled, his eyes shining. He was ready.

She moved her hips, angling into place, and, with one movement, took him inside her, their meeting like an exhalation of air—floating and forceful at the same time.

A collective moan escaped them both. The reuniting of two hungry bodies.

For a moment, she didn't move. Her hips remained frozen, the enjoyment of it all too perfect to be rushed.

"I'm okay," he whispered. "Make love to me."

A bloom of pleasure fanned out across her whole being, and she began to rock her hips, his hands on them to guide and to balance.

He moaned in appreciation. She reciprocated, a band of pure sensation uncoiling from her center.

Oh, have I missed this, she managed to think before rational thought became impossible.

Her movements increased, and Felix stayed with her, one of his hands leaving her hip and moving to her breast, his fingers playing with a nipple until it was rock hard, a sizzle racing up into her chest.

She let her head fall back, her eyes closing.

They were in perfect rhythm, their bodies overtaking their brains. Sabine marveled at her knees, their strength and power fueling her movements, her hips rolling faster and faster.

The uncoiling continued relentlessly. She knew it wouldn't be much longer until it unraveled completely. Oblivion was perilously near.

She opened her eyes, her need to make sure Felix was okay mixing with the desire to see him crest into orgasm.

She needn't have worried in the first place. Felix was strong enough for the action, and a moment later, his neck arched, his hair spiking over the pillow.

"Oh god!" he cried out, his voice cracking.

His body went stiff and still, even as Sabine ascended a moment later, the inky, decadent blankness of cumming enveloping her.

They shimmered and shook for a few moments more, and then her body, like an elastic band giving way, collapsed, her feverish skin falling on top of Felix.

His arms welcomed her, their hearts beating together.

For a while, neither spoke, and Sabine knew she would have to unbend her knees soon. She was amazed they hadn't protested yet.

"That... was the best medicine ever," Felix whispered into her ear as he playfully smacked her on the ass. "Thank you, nurse."

Sabine smiled into the pillow and whispered back.

"I'll be happy to give you a dose whenever you need it."

And she meant it. With her whole heart.

Chapter 32

Revelation

"Eight-letter word meaning person or thing to be imitated..." Sabine whispered to herself, chewing the end of her pencil. The crossword lay out before her, bright against the dark marble of Felix's kitchen counters.

Tea steeped next to her, a heady mix of herbs and spices that she bought from a cute little boutique online.

The answer didn't come, but surprisingly, it didn't frustrate her. She was oddly content. The only thing that disconcerted her was not knowing precisely why.

Her eyes drifted from the puzzle and out the window, where the afternoon played out in the green lushness of the garden and hills beyond.

Felix was napping in his bedroom, and Sabine waited for the casserole she was making to finish.

It was, in a word, idyllic. Downright domestic.

After making love a week before, the two had lain in each other's arms for hours. When night had arrived, they laid in bed and ate pizza like teenagers—Sabine only slightly anxious about the unhealthy option. Felix dismissed it, of course. He wanted to live, he'd said. And living meant eating pizza in bed with a pretty girl.

Who was Sabine to resist a thing like that?

Days whittled away, an easy routine forming between them.

Except for one thing—Sabine didn't know what it all meant. Was it supposed to mean something? Were they obligated to find a label for it?

Like his hospital stay, Sabine pushed such realities to the back of her mind, forcing herself to be ruggedly in the moment

For his part, Felix seemed only too happy to let things be.

So she stayed in a happy limbo, with her tea steeping and her crossword puzzle unfinished. It felt right. For now.

Ding dong.

Relaxed as she was, the harsh clatter of the doorbell made Sabine jump out of her skin.

She hurried to answer the door, not wanting Felix to be disturbed.

In doing so, however, she didn't take the precaution of checking the peephole. When she opened the door, she inwardly kicked herself for not doing so.

For there they were. The GGs. Festooned in perfume, pastels, and presents—just as they had in the ICU. Only now Sabine had no Dr. Watkins to beguile them away.

But now the door was open, she had no choice but to face them, hoping against hope she could at least keep their volume to a minimum.

That notion was shattered instantly.

"Heeyyyyy!" Grace cooed, sidling into the foyer, her perfume filling the air. "We have waited long enough! We just had to see how our dear Felix was doing!"

"Uhhh, yes, of course. Come on in," Sabine replied lamely, watching as the parade of GGs entered, their sandals slapping the tiles, their makeup glaring in the soft light of Felix's understated house.

"Let's head in here," Sabine directed, ushering them into the muted gray living room with its cream-colored sofa and matching chairs. Like everything else, it was sparse but tasteful. The bright colors and chirps of the GGs clashed harshly. Their balloons, cards, and gift bags gathered like a fungus around the coffee table.

Within a minute, all the GGs were arrayed on the furniture, an expectant air zipping around them.

All but one. Helen was notably absent.

Sabine busied herself bringing in lemonade and cookies hastily assembled on a tray. She was glad for the chore because it kept her out of their company a hair longer. It also gave her a chance to gather her thoughts.

What are they doing here? How can I get rid of them?

Soon enough, she couldn't eke out the catering duties any longer and was forced to sit down, a smile plastered on her face.

"Sooo... how are you all?" Sabine asked politely. "And where's Helen?"

The GGs bristled at the question. Shuddered, even. They looked to Grace to respond. Lips pursed, she replied.

"Licking her wounds, I expect. She's in time-out. And not just with us, but many people. I'm not sure whether she will stick around."

Sabine was confused.

"But why?"

Grace waved a hand. "We're not here to talk about her," she said derisively. "We're here to find out how Felix is doing. And how *you* are doing, of course..."

Grace's eyes drilled into Sabine, and her cheeks grew hot. Would she ever feel comfortable around this woman?

"He's doing great! He's just napping right now. But every day, he gets more and more on track. Pretty soon, he won't need me at all." Sabine said this with what she thought was a lighthearted tone, but the idea tugged at her. Soon they would have to come to terms; she would have to find out who he really was.

The GGs giggled, and Topaz replied, "From what I'm seeing, he'll never stop needing you."

Rebecca chimed in. "And I don't blame him, or *you*! He's a catch."

Sabine raised her hands in quick protest. "No! I just... I've only been helping out..."

Grace silenced her with a look. "Sabine, stop hiding it. We all know what's going on. It's as obvious as daylight. But, we don't blame you. We're all jealous of you, that's all."

"But I—"

"Felix is a hero, and we're all so grateful for him," Grace continued, delicately nibbling the edge of a cookie. "He saved us all."

"And got the guy caught, don't forget!" Ginny added. She waved a jade green finger in the air for emphasis.

Sabine sat up straighter.

"What guy? What's going on? I feel like I've been out of the loop," she said.

Grace shared a quick look with her girls and said, "Well, of course you have. And we left you alone until now, but it's time we thank Felix properly. And you, I suppose, for taking such good care of him."

Sabine sat back in her chair, suddenly weary. What were they talking about?

As if she could sense this, Grace cleared her throat.

"Felix figured out the scam and the scammer. It was Thad Varallo. Helen's son. That ghastly "presentation" for investments was merely a front for an off-shore account that funneled money back into Thad's own pocket. Some complicated back-and-forth that only geniuses would understand."

"Like Felix," Topaz interjected, smiling knowingly.

"Exactly," Grace concluded. "Like Felix. He combed through the records, made heaps of phone calls, and hounded everyone he knew from his old days. It was a mountain of trouble but he was able to figure it out, gather the evidence, and best of all, recoup the money." As she said it, Grace gave her shoulders a happy shrug.

"And Thad got arrested!" Rebecca chirped, her girlish glee at odds with her sentence.

"Felix did all that?" Sabine asked, dumbfounded.

Grace looked at her like she was a nitwit. "Yes. He did all that. Spent countless hours doing it. And must have gotten stressed in the process. I feel awful for what happened to him. All to get our money back."

"And to stop future scams," Topaz said. "This Thad has quite the past, apparently."

"And Helen...?" Sabine asked.

"We can't say what she did or didn't know, and right now, I don't care," Grace said with a thudding finality.

Sabine slumped even further into her seat, thunderstruck by the news. Felix had done all this—worked like a dog to get to the bottom of this scheme, and in the process had worn out his heart. What if he hadn't been saved? What if he hadn't made it?

A shudder ran through her, but also a feeling of relief. She looked at the GGs with a renewed sense of gratitude. They had brought her this news, after all. They knew what

Sabine hadn't—that Felix was a good man. That he'd worked to help the common good, at a huge personal cost.

She had to talk to Felix. Really talk to him.

Energy coursed through her.

"Anyone want some wine?" she asked, eager to get to know her new friends.

Chapter 33

Past Deeds

"**A**re they finally gone?" Felix asked, his eyes darting around the living room. It was dark now, only a few lamps creating soft blobs of light. Detritus littered the room: lipstick-stained wine glasses, crumpled-up tissue paper, and empty gift bags. The flock of balloons had drifted over to the corner. Plates with crumbs and tangled napkins dotted every surface.

Sabine laughed softly, her legs and back aching from hosting an impromptu party. The thought of cleaning up right now seemed monumental, akin to climbing a mountain. She sat, her feet tucked under her, on the couch.

"Yes, finally."

Though tired, Sabine was surprised how much she enjoyed the GGs company. Felix had joined them about twenty minutes in and was feted for several hours. The women knew how to chat, to laugh, and to keep the conversation from ever being boring.

Sabine and Felix exchanged glances throughout it all. They were never given space or time enough to really even talk to one another, but their smiles and looks told the other they were having a good time. That this was a welcome change to their once solitary world.

Now, however, Sabine welcomed the quiet. The hush of their bubble. The cocoon of just the two of them.

Except.

The GGs had celebrated Felix—praised him at a level that almost seemed god-like. Sabine enjoyed the adulations, but she couldn't fully participate. Something kept holding her back. A gnawing doubt that had to be either confirmed or expunged forever.

The time had come.

"That was fun," Felix said, nodding slowly. He sat on the chair nearest to Sabine, his hands sliding over each other as he cracked and flexed his long fingers. "I didn't expect that."

"Well, they really seemed to appreciate what you did for them. For everyone who was affected by that nonsense," Sabine replied, grateful for the on-ramp to this conversation. She had had no idea how to start it before.

Felix made a clicking sound. "Ah, it was nothing. I followed the breadcrumbs. That's all."

Sabine leaned forward, latching onto a sudden wave of bravery. She had to pursue this to the end.

"Felix. It doesn't sound like it was easy. And it doesn't sound like just anyone could do it. It takes someone special with numbers and banking to figure that out."

Felix looked at his hands. "Yes. Well."

"No, I'm serious. You're only the second person I have ever met who has that ability. The first was... he first was my late husband Colin."

She looked him in the eyes, realizing she had never really spoken to Felix about Colin before. Always afraid it would be like touching a flame. A destructive force that could ruin a good thing.

"Colin?" Felix asked, a note of caution in his voice.

"Yes. Colin Mayhew."

There was a moment. A hiccup of silence. Felix's face became an inscrutable mask. Then he spoke.

"Yes, Colin," he said, his voice hushed.

Sabine cocked her head. "You speak like you knew him."

Felix broke eye contact. "I did know him. Very well, in fact."

This was not something that Sabine could have predicted. An icy finger ran through her solar plexus.

"*You did?*"

"For years and years. We went to school together. Got our starts together. We were two peas in a pod."

Sabine stammered. "But... how? Colin never mentioned you. Never even said your name."

Felix filled his lungs and let out a labored sigh. "That doesn't surprise me. He had his reasons."

The icy feeling intensified, expanding in Sabine's chest like a fortress.

Now, it was all going to come out. Now, it was all going to be revealed that this man, who had rekindled so much in her, was a fraud. A con. Sabine's fingers tensed and her breathing went shallow.

"What reasons?"

Felix lifted his eyes to her. "Sabine, if I tell you, it's going to change things for you. Change what you know about people. What you knew about them."

As much as she wanted to rewind the clock and never broach this subject, Sabine knew she couldn't live in ignorance any longer. She had to know the truth.

In a small voice, she said, "Tell me, Felix."

He nodded and began to speak.

"I remember Colin telling me about you. When you first got together. He was so happy."

Sabine could only barely nod.

"He had just built a business based out of Houston, an equity trading firm."

Sabine nodded again. She recalled Colin talking about his frequent business trips, the stress he carried over its launch. It had been a difficult time in their budding relationship as they had less time to spend together, but Colin had assured her that things would settle after it was open.

And they had.

Until his health problems started not long after. It was a slow progression, but that was the beginning.

"The way he built it was... less than kosher, shall we say? He cut a few corners, made deals with the wrong people. Didn't do things in a way that would ensure the health of the organization. At some point, I told him, the auditors would come looking. He had built a business on quicksand."

Sabine tried to replay that time of her life in her head. Colin's late nights and his vague and curt answers whenever she asked how it was all going. His refusal to invite her to the launch party—telling her it was going to be boring.

Was that all a fiction?

"And... what was your part in all this?"

Felix clenched his jaw. "A few months in, the cracks started to appear, and he called me in a panic. I didn't know how bad it all was until he let me take a look at the books. It was bad. Like, almost federal prison bad."

Sabine's body went rigid. Her mind raced, scrambling to piece together memories from that time, her panic rising as they sifted together to form a complete picture. Colin had been tense with her in those days. Irritable for no reason, disappearing for hours and days on end, never fully answering her questions. Evasive and elusive.

She'd done her best to justify it into a comfortable narrative of the stress of a successful businessman.

"What did you do?" she asked.

"I did what I always do. I'm a forensic accountant. A regulator of sorts. I counseled him. Told him how to clean up his act. Set him straight. He didn't like it but knew he had to fly right if he was going to avoid prison time."

"And... he did what you told him to do?"

Felix nodded, but it seemed full of effort, like the act alone was exhausting.

"He did. But he didn't want to. And he hated the way I made him feel. He thought I judged him for his actions."

Sabine prodded. "And did you?"

"I tried not to," Felix confessed. "I could see how he was tempted. How the slow-and-steady-wins-the-race philosophy was tiring. And boring. But I didn't judge the man. Only his poor decisions."

"What happened?"

Felix went back to sliding his hands over each other, the soft swish of skin punctuating his words.

"He took my advice. Did what he was told. But our friendship was damaged. Probably the biggest damage he sustained, ironically. We were never the same. And, unfortunately, that's when his health started to..."

Like the reveal of the culprit at the end of any good mystery, Sabine felt the truth of Felix's words slam into place. It all made sense. All his actions—both with Colin and with Star Light—pointed to his integrity. A man with so much, he barely took any credit for it. Preferred to live in his actions rather than tout them.

No wonder Sabine had fallen for him. She just had to see past her own fears first. False fears at that.

She took his hands in hers.

"Why didn't you tell me this?"

One corner of Felix's lips curled upward. "I didn't think you'd believe me."

The sting of this truth lapped at her. Her own prejudices had prevented her from seeing things right in front of her. Sabine's conviction that Felix was a bad man because he had been aloof and quiet—she'd let her stubbornness cloud her to the deep, rich person he was.

And yet, some part of her had always known. Some part had gravitated towards him even as her mind resisted. Her core had always known this was a good man. A man she could trust utterly.

Her doubts evaporated, replaced with a profound sense of calm and gratitude.

And love.

"Thank you for telling me this. I'm sorry I ever doubted you."

A momentary question played across Felix's face—that he could be curious about her former misgivings, that he had the right to ask about them. But he didn't. He simply nodded again, content to leave Sabine's past prejudices to die on the vine.

"You're welcome."

She gave his hands a firm squeeze.

"Move in with me. I want you to have the better view."

She paused, looking at his face, his body, and his soul. Then she said, "And so will I."

He kissed her fingers softly.

"I would like that."

Epilogue

"Whoa. You weren't kidding," Hazel said, her lips curled in a mischievous grin. "They are out there in *force*. It's like a bag of Skittles exploded all over the chairs. So much color. Too much, really."

Sabine giggled swatting at her stepdaughter, well aware that the GGs had come out in their brightest finery to celebrate this day. Whether it was overcompensation for the loss of the most eligible bachelor at Star Light or because they genuinely felt happy for the couple was anyone's guess.

Sabine decided to be charitable and believe the GGs were happy for her. And for Felix, even if it meant he was off the table.

"Stop it. That's how they dress around here," Sabine replied, fiddling for the millionth time with her necklace and brooch. She couldn't keep any part of her body still. Nerves, excitement, abject terror, and something else—a deep well of calm had taken over her. She had trouble deciding which one she should pay attention to. They all took up space and energy, so she would just have to surrender to all of them at once. This day was charged, and she knew it.

A lightbulb epiphany lit up Hazel's face. "Do you think they'd let me write about them? It would be such a great feature about the culture and style of retirement in Florida."

"I think they would jump at the chance. Especially Grace," Sabine replied.

"Is she the one in blue? Hazel said, peeking through the gauzy curtains that shrouded her and Sabine from the group sitting in bright white chairs on Star Light's main lawn. Soothing strings music played over the speakers, and staff waiters milled about serving drinks.

The day was warm but not blisteringly hot. A gentle breeze blew over the guests, and the azure sky was dotted with happy, cherubic clouds.

In a word, it was perfect weather for a wedding.

While Hazel continued to spy on the assembling guests, Sabine couldn't help but marvel. It was all a blur since the day Felix and Sabine had cracked open their hearts and removed all doubts. She hadn't thought about marriage, but when Felix had casually mentioned it on a moonlit stroll two months prior, it felt like the most natural next step.

To spend the rest of their days together, each one caring for the other, was a no-brainer.

So why do I still feel so nervous?

"Move over, let me see," she said to Hazel, playfully poking the girl on the shoulder. Hazel shifted to the side, and Sabine looked at the gathering crowd.

It was hard to miss the GGs. They took up most of the front rows, their rainbow colors and bright fascinators drawing the eye. Others filling the chairs wore more muted grays and whites. Sabine was surprised at the turnout, but the ceremony was open to all Star Light residents, and who doesn't love a wedding?

But it wasn't the guests she was looking for. Her eye scanned to the front, where a simple lectern stood. There, in a pale lavender suit jacket and open-collar linen shirt, stood Felix. He wore sleek sunglasses, but they couldn't obscure his radiant expression. He had never been one to emote much in public, but it was obvious he was as giddy as she was.

Her nerves abated. Sabine wasn't nervous about the man she was about to marry. She was only nervous about the party. About being a good hostess.

But that was a small task in the greater scheme of things. Loving Felix was the real goal, and one she couldn't wait to start.

"I think they're ready for us," Hazel said, pulling back the curtain. "Are you?"

"Wait, Hazel," Sabine said, turning to face the young woman. Hazel looked at her with a mix of expectation and concern.

"Are you okay?" Hazel asked.

"I'm fine, but I want you to know something," Sabine said.

"Okay."

"No matter what, you are part of my life. Of *our* lives. Please know that. Please know that I loved your father very much and…" she drifted off, not sure how to finish her sentence. Her feelings for Colin were more nuanced than before. The knowledge of what he had done and how Felix had saved him had complicated things. But her love for him had been real, and she knew, deep down, that his had been real for her.

And now, miraculously, she'd been given a second

chance at love. Another chance to live a full and complete life.

Hazel kissed Sabine on the cheek.

"I know that. And I know Dad would always want you to be happy. He's smiling on us now. I bet he's the one that sent this weather."

Tears welled up in Sabine's eyes. She mumbled her thanks.

Hazel nodded.

"Now, get out there and make it official before one of those flamingos out there takes him from you."

Sabine laughed, her tears turning to joy.

"Gotcha."

Together, they pulled back the curtain and stepped out into the sun.

Heads turned. The music swelled.

The two women made their way down the grassy aisle, each holding a simple bouquet of peonies, the scent drifting over the crowd.

In the periphery, Sabine noticed the smiles, the encouraging looks, and the beginning of happy tears in her guests.

But her true sight only had one focus. Felix.

The Silver Hammer himself.

He removed his glasses and looked at her, his face open with love and gratitude.

"I love you," he mouthed, his eyes shining.

She kissed her fingers and blew them towards him, wafting on the scent of peonies.

"I do too," she mouthed back.

Three more steps and she would be at his side. Their new life was about to begin.

She could hardly wait.

Acknowledgments

Thanks to Dan Hodge and Trashcan for letting me pitch an idea that I thought was utter nonsense. You saw something there and encouraged me to believe in it.

Thanks to you, the Reader, for jumping in, embracing whatever this world is and hopefully, being hungry for more. I hope to never disappoint.

To my many friends who have expressed support, surprise, or a combination of both when they realize I've written a book (or two).

Finally, thanks to my husband Damon and my son Julian for giving me a quiet space to write, the encouragement to do so, and the listening ear when I needed it.

And of course, who can forget the warmth (and distraction) of my cats, Rosie, Riggles and the irascible Toast? Love you all – always.

About the Author

Charlotte Northeast spent time during the pandemic lurking in the shadows of ghostwriting but is now proud to be out in the open. She has written books across several different genres: rom-com, sci-fi, religious and fantasy. Her career started in the theatre where she is an actor, director and writer.

She is one quarter of the writing team of *The Complete Works of Jane Austen, Abridged* (also a performer). Her adaptation of Thomas Heywood's *Fair Maid of the West Parts 1 and 2*, was an audience favorite, and a critical success for the Philadelphia Artists' Collective (PAC) in 2015.

Since then, she has adapted Fletcher's *Tamer Tamed*, and been a devising mind behind several shows, including *You Shouldn't Be Doing What You're Doing On That Ladder* and *Citrus Andronicus*.

Author of the **Small Town Talk Series** and the **Assisted Sinning Series**. Charlotte lives in Collingswood, NJ with her husband, son and two ridiculous cats.